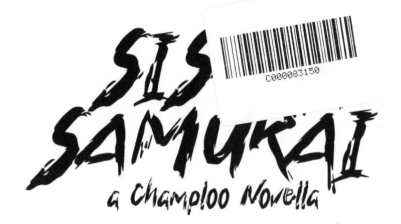

SIS
SAMURAI
a Champloo Novella

SISTAH SAMURAI

a Champloo Novella

TATIANA OBEY

ビオー

 WANDERLORE PUBLISHING LLC

www.tatianaobey.com

Cover illustration by Félix Ortiz
Visual Glossary Illustration by Alayna (_kviio_)

Wanderlore Publishing LLC
325 North St Paul Street, Ste 3100
Dallas, TX 75201

v 1.03

ISBN: 979-8-9856649-7-3 (trade pbk.)
ISBN: 979-8-9856649-6-6 (e-book)
ISBN: 979-8-9856649-8-0 (hardcover)

to the Black women who have raised me,
who have carried me, and who have held me,
this is my love letter to you

To my fam: Welcome home.

To everyone else: You are a guest in this house.
Mind your manners.

VISUAL GLOSSARY

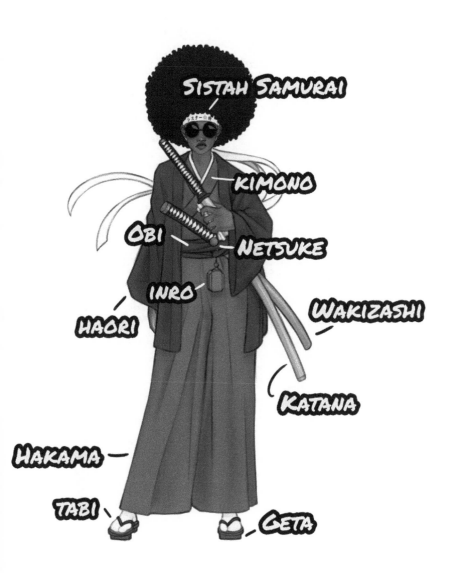

Sistah Samurai

KIMONO

OBI

NETSUKE

INRO

WAKIZASHI

HAORI

KATANA

HAKAMA

TABI

GETA

THE PLAYLIST

SISTAH SAMURAI MIX VOL. 2

10. NIGGAS GOT ME F'D UP—AMANDA SEALES
11. BLK GIRL SOLDIER
    JAMILA WOODS
12. LADIES FIRST—QUEEN
    LATIFAH FT. MONIE LOVE
13. FORMATION
    BEYONCE
14. BREAK FOOL
    RAH DIGGA
15. FOREVER—SA-ROC
16. BAG LADY—ERYKAH
    BADU
17. FINAL FORM—SAMPA THE GREAT
18. FEEL THE NEED—ERYN ALLEN KANE
19. GIRL SAMURAI LULLABY—RAH DIGGA

BONUS SONGS: SAY HE-
HOLY—JAMIL
ON MY MA

SISTAH SAMURAI MIX VOL. 1

1. BREAK MY SOUL—BEYONCE
2. SOLDIER OF LOVE
   SADE
3. BLACK GIRL MAGIK
   SAMPA THE GREAT
4. SAVAGE (REMIX)
   MEGAN THEE STALLION
   FT. BEYONCE
5. RESPECT—
   ARETHA FRANKLIN
6. SNATCHED—BIG BOSS VETTE
7. CRANES IN THE SKY
   SOLANGE
8. SECRET SERVICE
   LEIKELI47
9. LA DIASPORA—NITTY
   SCOTT FT. ZAP MAMA

CHAPTER 1

BREAK MY SOUL

I knew it was gonna be one of *those* days when I forgot my glasses.

Look now, I don't really need them. I'm not dependent on them like some newborn at their momma's tits. I am a grown-ass woman. They're just nice to have around, you know? For just in case purposes. But mostly all I do is run the same errands every day, and I don't need no help to see the ground I've walked a thousand times before.

I squinted, careful to align the sharp edge of my wakizashi against my forearm. I trailed along yesterday's barely healed scar and without fuss, sliced another shallow cut into the skin. I collected the welled blood with practiced ease, wiped at the sweat gathered beneath my headband, and glared at the sun until my eyes watered—probably why I needed those damn glasses in the first place. Then I exchanged my blood, sweat, and tears for a single vial of ink.

The ink gleamed a mighty shade of incandescent ebony. No speckles or air bubbles from what I could see. Tamashii ink is an extraction of a person's soul, they say. If so, the color of mine must be blackity black black black.

The proud inksmith grouched at my scrutiny—a dance

we do every time, the motions rote and predictable like a line dance. He could pretend at offense all he wanted, but I was checking this ink. After all, it was always the one time you don't that comes to bite you in the ass. By now, the master inksmith knew that this was something I had to do, just as I knew that his hemming and hawing was something he had to do. So we danced our dance like old begrudging partners.

He was a tough old thing, with fingers like gnarled roots and skin like stubborn bark. The only softness he had to him was his eyebrows, which clung to him like white cottonwood seeds. Sometimes I wondered if one good blow could scatter them right off his face the way kids wished on a dandelion. How many wishes you think he held in them fuzzy brows?

Ink boiled in the back of his open-air shop, carrying a perfume of apricot blossoms seeping into the earthen-plaster and woven bamboo walls. Straw-knotted sumi sticks hung from the ceiling to dry. Although selling tamashii ink was quite the lucrative business, the inksmith still practiced that old traditional art. Liver-spotted hands kneaded passion and pride into a ball of glue and pine soot.

As he worked, his foot twitched, knocking the wooden frames that were scattered along the ground. His knee bounced higher and higher with every second I lingered over the ink.

A smirk pulled at my lips. The wizened master guffawed. Sometimes, the humor of a younger and more mischievous life possessed me, stealing away the years like a gust of wind smelling of my parents' sunflower fields.

"Shouldn't you be going, Sistah Samurai? Don't you got some place to be?"

Tsk. I certainly didn't need no reminder of how life has become one errand after another. There was never any time for fun anymore, nor time for teasing old inksmith that grumped too much like my former sensei. He did have a point, though. Even I could recognize when the dance had gone on for too long. No more time for encores. No more time for freestyling. Not even time for a little wiggle.

With a sigh, I gave the master inksmith a parting nod. He gave me a respectful one in turn.

Till next time.

I deposited the ink within the stitched pocket of my obi. My ride-or-dies, my katana and wakizashi, rode shotgun in pink lacquered sheathes on my hip. I plucked the sunglasses from my 'fro, cleaned off the grease with the edge tip of my haori, and refitted them over my eyes.

I see you looking at me. I know what you're thinking: this girl done left her glasses at home, but she sure did remember to grab her shades. Well, yeah, 'cause they make me look like a baaaad motherfucker.

So mind ya business.

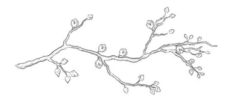

CHAPTER 2

SOLDIER OF LOVE

My steel-plated getas click-clacked along the petal-coated cobblestones of Chigakure. This place was one of those boondock villages tucked out of the way of the main roads. Or at least it used to be. Now, bamboo shacks brawled hinoki constructions for space along the crowded thoroughfare. This senile village wasn't ready for the population explosion that bloated its walls, often creaking and straining like an elder complaining of too many grandchildren in their house.

I didn't blame anybody for seeking shelter at one of the last places not yet decimated by demons, but what I didn't get was how folks *assumed* this village was under the protection of the Sistah Samurai who often patroned its businesses. Look, I had a bad hip and my knees hurt more days than not. My time of hero-ing was long behind me. I've finally stopped rolling my eyes at the way everyone bowed as I walked past. They did it so often. But I was no different than any of the rest of them. I was out here surviving like everybody else. They called me Sistah Samurai, but in truth, I was just a tired woman tired of being tired.

Back in the day, a samurai's duty was to serve as retainers and stewards of their daimyo's feudal domain, but that way of life was shredded to pieces when the demons overran the capital, Edolanta, seven years ago during the Empress's coronation. With the death of the Empress and the gathered daimyos, the attack had shattered the political system of Buredoshima into lawless territories and up-start warlords. The Sistah Samurai had accompanied their lieges to the capital and on that fateful day, I had lost them all.

I should have been there. I should have been standing pauldron to pauldron by their side, but I . . . was no hero.

The clan had acted as a dam against the demon hoard, but now the floodgates were burst open. The world changed overnight, and most folks were still scrambling to find a life raft—and Chigakure happened to be that rickety boat in a sea of horrific darkness. The only difference between me and everybody else was that I've got a katana to help me row, but most times, it didn't keep me moving forward none.

I turned back.

Thought I saw something move in the corner of my eye. I stilled and watched the sun stretch the shadows of old friends playing spades under the awnings. They bowed their heads under my scrutiny, and one of them offered to let me join their game. Another offered up their son instead. I politely declined their offers and continued on my way.

Hmph. Can't trust those shadows sometimes.

The sun was higher than when I arrived through the village gates and now stupidly blazed heat onto my shoulders. The afro provided some measure of shade, and the headband kept the sweat from my eyes, but I was feeling the heat through my layers of clothing. It was warmer down here from where I started up the mountain; either that or it was one of those hot flashes my granny used to warn me about. Desperate for relief, I shrugged off my haori and wrapped the sleeves around my waist. Underneath, I wore a faded and lived-in black kimono while everyone else in the village had already donned their spring yukatas. The bright floral prints decorated the streets like spring shower rainbows, and I shoved through those rainbows like a thundercloud.

For a moment, I hovered beneath the cool shade of a sprawling cherry blossom tree, which was always posing like a dancer at the center of a courtyard I regularly cut through to reach the main road. Thick white rope encircled the sacred tree like a decorative obi, and the wind shook the branches, rustling them like tambourines.

I don't remember the last time I paused to appreciate the transient blossoms. Probably not since I was a young girl when my Sistahs and I would enjoy the hanami festivals after sword practice.

All of a sudden, names and faces bombarded my thoughts. A rush of memories hit like a well-delivered blow to the solar plexus. I turned away from the tree, bowed my head, and focused on breathing through the nauseous weight on my stomach. I squeezed my eyes shut to the creeping shadows, to find the taste of springtime dango on my tongue, the smell of takoyaki hushpuppies popping and sizzling on the grill, and the sound of girlish giggles bubbling and bursting in my ear. Sometimes, in those moments when I wade through the knowledge that I was the only one left, a vague out-of-body experience came over me and I became a ghost haunting the living, anchored only to the present by the past.

A gust showered pink petals down on my hair.

I charged away from the tree, but those damn petals seemed to trail after me, falling into my kimono collar every time I turned my head. I clutched my hand around the hilt of my katana, over the pink outer wrapping of the ray skin, as if that was going to do any good. Still, I kept a grip on that hilt until my beating heart slowed to a ballad.

I hated spring. I hated cherry blossoms. I hated pink.

When I reached the main road, I braced myself for the blast of color. Cherry blossom trees lined both sides of the thoroughfare, their branches arching overhead like childhood friends holding hands. I begrudgingly walked beneath the pink floral cloud, wary that at any moment, it could all topple down and suffocate me.

What made it worse were all the children running around, not watching where they were going, and getting underfoot. They were every shade of melanin you could imagine, from black pine to white birch, representative of the diaspora who have fled from all over the island to find refuge in this small village. They filled the air with their shrieking as they weaved through the crowds. One hopscotched into my path, a young girl with missing teeth, an Ankara-patterned yukata, and hair split into two ponytail puffs by colorful butterfly baubles.

Her heels skidded along the paved road and stopped with a jerk. She would have collided with my legs if I hadn't taken a step back. The girl looked up with an obvious apology on her lips but seemed to have gotten distracted. Her mouth dropped open in awe as she stared at me, as if my halo of hair marked me as some sort of goddess worthy of worship. I snorted. Before I could shoo her off, a *tap tap tadum* of drums distracted us both.

I grabbed the girl by the shoulder and firmly pulled her back with the rest of the crowd as the drums approached. The drummers led a procession of gossiping geishas through the crowd. Their attendants shaded the young women with paper parasols as they walked the streets to enjoy the cherry blossoms. Dramatic and voluminous yukatas blanketed body types of all sizes. They wore their hair fancy-like in elaborate braided up-dos pinned by delicate kanzashi hairpins. Their faces were painted cobalt black, highlighted further by sparkling gold lipstick and swooping eyeliner. Usually, I'd roll my eyes at the spectacle, but I knew the peacocking was all a part of their hustle.

"I want to be like you," the little girl whispered while the crowd admired and gawked over the geisha.

"No, you don't," I responded automatically, and told her, "Become a geisha. Theirs is a respectable practice. You'll learn to sing, and dance, and play various instruments. It's an honest living."

"I want to become like you," the little girl said, even more insistent. "My dad was killed by demons. I want to become a samurai so that I can protect my family and everyone that I love."

For a moment, I saw another little girl in her face—a little girl so angry and so vengeful after stumbling upon the corpses of her family in the sunflower fields. She had lost her parents, her grandmother, and her little brother that day. The demons had consumed their souls and left their bodies behind for the crows.

But that was a long time ago. Anger was for the youth, and I was mostly just tired now, so tired of burying folks. I wanted to shake the girl and warn her that loss was never-ending, and that no matter how hard we try to prevent it, cherry blossoms always fall.

Before I could crush the little girl's naivete, a voice called out, "There you are."

I swiveled in the direction of that baritone voice. I saw the head over the crowd before I saw the rest of him. He was that tall. Once people saw him coming this way, they parted for him, not because they were intimidated by the broad shoulders and muscled physique that the formless robes did little to hide, but out of respect for the order he belonged to. The chain medallions, the calligraphy staff, and the white silk du-rag that flowed to his ankles clearly identified him as belonging to the Sacred Order of Brotha Monks. They often did charity work in the area and were held in high regard among the villagers.

I didn't recognize this one, and I've been visiting Chigakure for some time now. He must be new to the village, but not new to the order judging by the number of chains around his neck. I've worked with enough Brothas to know that every chain marked a year of service, with medallions signifying a particularly distinguished year. This guy had fifteen chains and five medallions, higher than the Head Monk currently stationed in the village. It immediately made me wonder if something was going on and . . . Nope. None of my business. They could be organizing a cipher to practice their haikus for all I care.

"Your mom is looking for you, young lady," the monk said. He grabbed the girl by the shoulder as if knowing at any moment she could be spirited away. "She reported you missing at the temple. This is the second time this week."

"But-"

"No, buts," the monk reprimanded. "Your mom cares for you too much to be worrying her, you feel me?"

The girl searched the crowd, probably for those friends of hers she was playing with, but seeing them long gone, her shoulders drooped in surrender. "Fine."

The monk nodded in approval. He then looked at me and was not all as thunderstruck as the little girl had been. Wouldn't be surprised to learn that the villagers have been gossiping about me to the newcomers. He gave me an acknowledging nod up. "Sistah."

"Brotha," I acknowledged, nodding up in turn.

The Brotha Monks and Sistah Samurai often disagreed regarding different methodologies and approaches to dealing with the demons. The Brothas were often too busy trying to figure out where the demons came from to actually deal with the demons clawing at their faces, but in the end, we were in this fight together. I held no grudges against them, except for the fact that most of them were still alive . . . And curiously congregating in the village. We stood staring at each other, awkwardly. What was *he* waiting for?

"You're new," I said, folding to my damned curiosity.

"A refugee, just like everyone else."

Straight lying out of his neck. I debated if I should call him out on it, which led to another uncomfortable silence. Even the little girl, who was looking between us with some confusion, blurted, "Just ask her out already."

He stepped closer to me, as if to whisper something, but that was quite close enough. I didn't like anyone past my wakizashi range that I didn't invite in. I drew back, reestablishing that comfortable range of distance, and he looked at me with further confusion. Didn't know why he was actin' so confused. You never step into a swordswoman's space without cause.

"You got it?" he asked, a tinge of desperation in his voice now. "Why haven't you gone to the temple with it?"

"Have what? All I know is if you step to me like that again, I'm gonna strangle you with your damn chains." I said, tired of all this. "I don't know what you're talking about. You've got the wrong person. Whoever you think I am, I am not her. How many other Sistah Samurai you know out here with an afro?"

"I . . . " Something in my words must've clicked, for his eyes widened. "Nah. You right. I mistook you for somebody else. My deepest apologies, Sistah. If you would allow me to treat you to lunch, I could clear up the confusion, know what I mean?"

"Ha! It is a date!" The little girl said triumphantly.

I honestly didn't know if this dude was sincere or if this was the weirdest pick-up line I have ever heard. Either way, I didn't have time for this.

"Don't bother me again," I threatened, before walking away into the dispersed crowd now that the geishas had passed. I had more important things to do than to figure out the monks and their cryptic bullshit. But still . . .

What the du-rag fuck?

CHAPTER 3

BLACK GIRL MAGIK

Whatever was going on with the monks, I decided to let it go. More often than not, those staff wielding pacifists were harmless. Besides, I had more pressing matters to attend to, like the incessant grumbling in my stomach. I scanned over the crowd for a place to eat, over the various heads of hair that were braided, loc'd, coiled, twisted, weaved, pressed, picked, curled, gelled, and blowed out.

Most restaurants had a line of people snaking out the doorway, but I wasn't much a fan of crowds. A gaggle of accents congregated around signs that advertised discounted prices on well-done sushi and tempura fried chicken. But I didn't have a taste for none of it.

The once-rural village of Chigakure was nowhere near a match for the chaotic glittering metropolis of Edolanta, but I didn't think anything could ever rival the magnitude of that coercive capital. They say you could find anything among the floating world—from the bright neon of the red-light district, the seductive company of high-ranking oirans with nails the length of their hairpins, the hoots and hollers of bombastic kabuki performances, and the dance clubs with DJs that talked over the track and bass so loud it shook the walls.

But what I remembered most was the food.

You could taste the whole of Buredoshima in that one city—from yuzu jerk chicken to taiyaki waffles to upside-down matcha cake to miso butter cookies. But today, Edolanta was nothing but a graveyard, leaving me behind to perpetually mourn its culinary spirit.

So far, only one restaurant met my exacting standards.

I stepped off the main street, toward the warren of dirt roads where buildings rubbed each other's shoulders for room. Every time I visited Chigakure, there was a new street or pathway that made the old village maps look as if someone had sneezed on them and shuffled everything haphazardly askew.

There used to be a street that led straight to my favorite restaurant, but someone had plopped a house in the middle of it and that street didn't exist anymore. Instead, I took three right turns, passed underneath a roughshod bridge, navigated through a hybrid bakery-tailor-barbershop monstrosity mishmash to reach the plaza that had been five steps from where I started if I could walk through walls.

At the very least, there was no line spilling out the restaurant's door since only determined locals ever visited it nowadays. The restaurant had been operating in this village for years, but all the new buildings that had sprung up around it made it difficult for newcomers to find.

The maze of hastily constructed buildings had also become a playground for pickpockets and wily scam artists, but that was the extent of the worst crime in Chigakure, and a simple glare served to stop most up-to-no-gooders in their tracks. For now, the most distinctive feature of the haphazard maze was the graffiti murals of infinity symbols that served as helpful markers to find your way.

Paper talismans dangled outside of the restaurant's doorway, and I noted that the ink of them had almost faded.

They would need to be replaced soon.

I entered through the divided curtains, and the wonderful smell of spice flooded my senses. The chef nodded once I came through the entranceway.

He said, with that childhood Edolanta accent he refused to let die, "Your table is ready, Sistah Samurai. I'll prepare your usual. I gotchu."

The restaurant was far from empty, but it wasn't crowded either—filled with regulars that acknowledged me with a downward nod.

I sat at the empty table located underneath one of the circular windows. It was always conveniently empty at this time of day. Some might even say it had become *my* table. I unbelted Fuck-Around and Find-Out, my katana and wakizashi, and placed the blades along the bench beside me. I sat with my back to the door to block out distractions and sat forward toward the window, taking advantage of how the sun washed over the table's wooden surface at this time of day. I liked the greater visibility and how the shifting light made it easier to mind the time. Too often, it was so easy for time to get away from me. I found that it could be a fast, wily creature, and I was getting too old to keep chasing it.

I pinned my shades back into my 'fro. Then, I lined the table with my tools from the lacquered inro that sat against my thigh: a stack of fiber paper, a long slender calligraphy brush, and the stout ink vial I had received from the inksmith earlier.

First things first: I used my wakizashi to scratch a line into the vial—the line I should never cross.

Then, I swept back the sleeves of my kimono, closed my eyes, and took a concentrated breath. With a practiced careful motion, I dipped the brush into the ink.

As one of the Illustrious Sistah Samurai, I was taught the secret arts of shodou-jujutsu. The practice evolved from the ofuda tradition, but instead of invoking the blessings of a god, the tamashii ink invoked a person's soul. Most of the hawkers on the road selling talismans to desperate travelers were butchers of the art, and every crude attempt made me wince.

As I danced ink across the paper, I could hear my old sensei criticizing every brush stroke. I could almost feel that old twinge of pain rap across my knuckles back when I wasted a drop of ink. A mournful smile stamped my face as I worked.

I used four strokes to write the kanji for FIRE (火) onto the paper. More complicated kanji required more ink. Any wobble in the strokes made the spell less effective. An egregious mistake could cause the spell to backfire. You could create talismans with any type of tamashii ink, but there was no ink more effective to use than the ink made from your own soul.

After I finished creating the talisman, I placed it aside and started on the next: EARTH (土), WATER (水), and TRAP (囲). I allowed myself a powerful one, just in case—LIGHTNING (雷).

I glanced at the ink vial. The level of ink had diminished quite a bit, nearing the line I had scratched onto the outside of it. I couldn't risk going any lower, needing to reserve that ink for a later task.

I created only one more talisman—PROTECTION (保).

I slid the six talismans into the press of my obi, ordered by stroke count to easily grab the one I needed during a fight. Once I cleared the table, the chef's son came over with my usual order. The kid was as thin and gangly as the locs bundled atop his head. He poured me a cup of water, with charcoal sticks thudding against each other in the pitcher. He set before me a large bowl of spicy miso ramen and side dishes of collard green miso and tempura okra. The ramen's steaming vapors warmed my face and cleared my sinuses.

It was such a masterful piece of art: brilliant gold at

the center of the halved boiled egg, chopped bright green onions and the dark green seaweed, beautiful brown braised pork belly, and golden bamboo shoots. All presented atop a rich marigold broth.

I looked forward to this moment every single day. It was the one opportunity where I could sit down, savor the time, and enjoy myself.

I picked up the provided chopsticks, gave thanks for the food, and took that exultant first bite. Spicy umami boldness painted my tongue. I slurped it loudly, joining the chorus of the other patrons in the room and drowning out the local shamisen player who plucked a slow jam on the instrument's three strings in the corner.

This was some good shit. I didn't even have to add hot sauce to it.

A set of unfamiliar footsteps plodded through the doorway. Frayed sandals slapped against rough, calloused heels. Not a regular.

"Hand over all of your ink," the newcomer demanded. The chef dropped his knife with a clatter. The young server stuttered, knees a'knocking.

Immediately, I could feel the eyes of the restaurant's patrons land on my back, itching at it as if I had forgotten to put on lotion. *No. Nope.*

I didn't have the time to be involved. I wasn't some wandering hero, and I was already confined to a tight schedule. This was the only time I had to myself, and I was going to enjoy my lunch, dammit.

So leave me alone.

CHAPTER 4

SAVAGE (REMIX)

Then again . . . This *was* my favorite ramen joint.

All eyes in the restaurant watched my every motion, but I took my time using a cloth napkin to dab the ramen broth from my mouth that burned deliciously at the corner of my lips. I took one, two, three refreshing sips of water before finally bringing my hands to the table to stand up. I glanced over my shoulder at the scrawny thief and his two friends.

If these aspiring thieves were out here demanding ink, that meant they were involved in something bigger than just petty crime. The lot of them wielded petty knives and wore pink bandannas over their faces. What was this? Some new gang I didn't know about that went around stealing ink and shouting about breast cancer awareness?

The ramen chef glanced in my direction, and the attention of the trio's apparent leader soon followed. The thief glared at me where I stood and gave a pubescent trill of a growl, "What the fuck do you want, *you old bitch*?"

The shamisen stopped playing. The patrons froze

with ramen hanging down their chins. A cat meowed. The entire restaurant held a collective breath.

I didn't bother grabbing Fuck-Around and Find-Out. No point wasting good ink or dulling an edge on these squids. I reached for a different tool instead.

"Did you fucking hear me? I said—" The thief choked. Too bad the rest of his words were garbled on the bloody chopstick sticking out of his throat.

I had some damn good aim.

Blood spurted as he toppled backward. The poor patrons close to the shower scrambled away from their tables with ramen bowls hoarded in their arms, faces speckled with blood and hot broth. The thief's friends shouted in alarm, pointed, and then charged toward me.

I kicked an empty table between us. It skidded forward and slammed into their knees. They stumbled, and I kindly helped their momentum by grabbing the closest one by his manbun and slamming him into the wood. With the second chopstick between my fist, I punched through the man's ear. A squelched pop. The light in his eyes burst like a shattered oil lamp.

The last thief hesitated where she stood, unable to decide if she should help or run. I raised a pointed eyebrow, daring her to try. Proving to have more intelligence than her friends, she tripped backward and raced out the door. No doubt to blab to her employer about what had happened here.

A frown marred my expression as I tried to make sense of it all. Most criminal activity in Chigakure was rather benign, and as far as I knew, free of the organized crime that had infected Edolanta before it collapsed.

But . . . Chigakure might just be a big city now, or quickly getting there. I noted the pinpricks on each of the corpses' wrists and the black fingernails that identified the thieves as having worked at the local ink factory. I stripped the corpse, the one with a chopstick through his brain, of his pink scarf and studied the paisley design on the cotton.

"Heard one of dem warlords trying to move into town," one of the restaurant patrons, the nice man who always carried his cat everywhere, explained. That fluffy cat was currently curled atop the man's green, yellow, and red conical bamboo hat. "Lot of businesses being robbed of dey ink lately, nah mean? Peoples sayin' he calling himself the Pink Diamond Warlord."

Never heard of him. No surprise, though, as it was hard to keep up with what warlord was in charge of this territory or that. Most of them were nothing but upstart roadside robbers when Edolanta fell, but there was something in particular about this one that rubbed me the wrong way.

I crumpled the pink bandanna in my fist.

Pink was the color of The Clan of Illustrious Sistah Samurai. Everyone knew that. But the clan was gone now, and the color was free to be reinvented and re-imagined. Still, I never thought someone would have the gall to distort it this way—to change a color associated with power and protection to one of fear and oppression. Despite all my own complicated hang-ups about the color, this didn't feel right. This was my Sistahs' legacy someone was fucking with.

And yet, I forced myself to bite down on those sentimental emotions. I couldn't afford to be no justice warrior. I was nothing but a woman with a tight schedule to keep, and all I wanted to do was mind my business. After all, I had already failed my Sistahs so much; what was one more failure? What was one more snowball on that mountain?

I returned to my now *cold* ramen.

The son, at behest of the chef, brought me over a

new steaming bowl of ramen. Bless him. The boy even gave me a clean pair of chopsticks, although he was a little hesitant as he did so. The musician continued her song, a bluesy enka this time.

"Thank you, Sistah Samurai," the boy said, all pimply and gangly. I winced when he slapped a rag down on the floor and began scrubbing up the blood. One of the patrons, the one that had spoken earlier, assisted in moving the bodies. I couldn't help but wonder what would happen to the young server once a warlord moved into town. It was youth like him that got swept up in the ensuing violence first.

Several of the patrons resumed eating, but nothing was the same as before.

The ramen hit different. The music sounded more solemn. The air felt heavier, tinged with the iron of blood that normally tainted the air outside the village walls. Despite the village's best efforts, violence had swept in to ruin the fragile peace I had always known would pop eventually.

I slurped down my ramen.

Ugh. Who was this so-called warlord extorting my favorite restaurant? Slurp. Who dared to have the audacity to mess with my not-so-little-anymore village? Slurp. Whose lackeys had no respect for their elders? Slurp. Who dared to rebrand *my* color? Slurp.

I didn't have time for this. *Clink.*

I looked down at my empty bowl of ramen. I liked to savor lunch. It was the only time of day that I could slow down and enjoy a brief peace, but look at that— now I was finished early. I glanced at the thinning light from the window and huffed.

Fuck it. I got time today.

CHAPTER 5

RESPECT

The patrons paid for their ramen with a single drop of ink before shuffling out of the restaurant. Gone were the days when wages and trade goods were paid for with sacks of rice or with copper and iron coins. Now, tamashii ink has become the world's most single important commodity. In the early years after the fall of the capital, I saw parents selling their babies, children betraying their parents, and siblings stabbing each other in the back for just a vial of the ink's protective power.

Desperation made monsters of us all.

Most ink was mass-produced in factories, such as the one our ambitious thieves worked in. The factories produced enough ink for the village to keep talismans plastered outside of everyone's homes and the village walls, but talismans made from mass-produced ink were less efficient than the specialty ink I received from the inksmith and, when activated, only lasted a few hours.

It was procedure for the village guards to activate the talismans during a demon sighting, but that was how they lost the capital. The demon surge had lasted longer than the number of talismans they had on hand. Then the walls fell, and those defending them fell soon afterward.

Most villages learned from that tragedy. Ink rose higher in demand, and now, most of the citizenry was armed with talismans of their own in case the walls and their defenders should ever fall again. I certainly understood their anxiety and distrust. After the capital, I didn't trust any talismans that weren't made from my own brushstrokes.

"You're finished early today, Sistah Samurai," the chef said as I stomped toward the door. For a moment, panic crossed his face, as if I would forget our unspoken agreement. Okay, fine, maybe I was about to forget. That was how much those punks have thrown me off balance.

"Hn," I responded, refusing to acknowledge that I had almost forgotten about him. I reached into my sleeve and retrieved one of the talismans I had created earlier, the one I had written with the kanji for PROTECTION. I affixed it to the doorframe. The talismans were activated by nothing but intention, but it was a task that many failed when under stress, fear, or panic.

I activated the talisman, and the ink glowed a brilliant gold. In twenty-four hours, the ink would eventually fade and disappear from the paper entirely, ending the spell. If the demons were ever to breach the gates while I was away, I had no doubt that this restaurant would be the only building left standing . . . and the inksmith's shop. Probably. If the old man didn't forget to activate his talismans again.

"See you tomorrow!" The chef called after me.

I nodded and exited through the door without breaking stride. I put on my shades and glared at the smoke snaking through the sky, using it as a point of reference to navigate through the warren of mangled streets.

Of course, those punks had to come from the ink factory. It was admittedly the first place I would take control over if I were some upstart warlord looking to move in and take over territory. Honestly, it was all rather unimaginative, but the tactics often worked. The factory had a habit of overworking its employees, forcing them to toil long hours for little wages and gleefully took advantage of the surge in refugees. It was a place rife with the potential for corruption.

The grumpiness I felt while rushing through lunch was momentarily forgotten as I felt a tingle of excitement skipping on my toes. I rarely got the opportunity to deviate from my usual routine—leave home, buy ink, eat lunch, return home, and kill the occasional demon along the way. Then I wake up and do it all over again.

I knew I shouldn't be so excited about the detour, but when the days have become mechanical and rote, it was nice when something blunted the routine. Except those days looking to kill me. I could do without those.

I must admit, this place wasn't as small as the quaint village I first discovered four years ago. The factory itself was also bigger than I remembered. It had gone from the bamboo shack the village elders had hastily erected to produce ink faster than the inksmith, to a privately funded metal behemoth.

I entered through the open industrial doors of the factory and scrunched my nose at the stench of sweat and unwashed bodies. On one half of the factory floor, the paid volunteers rotated between various extraction stations where they bled, cried, and sweated into various containers. Their faces gaunt and their frames thin as their souls were violently wrung out of them.

On the other side, the workers chopped pine wood and burned the pieces in a large industrial wood-burning stove. Then they poured the burned soot, nikawa, musk, and the collected soul essences into large grinding machines that took three workers to crank. And the noise was something awful, like some annoying child cracking ice right into your ear.

After all that grinding, they stirred, cooled, and strained

the mixture in large vats and repeated that same process over the next few days until they had vials of *inferior* tamashii ink. Many of the workers have worked in the factory for so long that the ink had stamped their skin a cobalt black and permanently stained their fingernails with an ebony polish.

The factory floor was a lot of sensory information to take in at once, but I had already identified all the exits and all the impediments in my path.

The young female goon that had fled the restaurant was speaking with the foreman at the back of the factory, surrounded by shelves of neatly bottled ink. Over the girl's shoulder, the foreman spotted me and fled toward the stairs, upturning tables and shattering ink bottles on the way. He ran into his office on the second floor and slammed the door behind him with the heaviness of a beat drop.

Two of the foreman's bodyguards stepped into the space that the foreman had hastily vacated. They each unsheathed their respective katanas. I huffed and pinned my sunglasses back into my 'fro and was disappointed to find the lighting within the factory as dark and grim as when I had my shades on.

One of the bodyguards placed a talisman along their blade. The ink flared gold, and the blade ignited. Tendrils of flames spiraled around the metal.

Cute.

I unsheathed my katana, and the sound of it whispered sweetly, like a song you leaned in to hear and savor. Then, I reached into my obi to retrieve the talisman marked with the kanji for FIRE and pasted it along the curved steel.

I winked, and my katana belted a roaring inferno. My ink had produced a glorious blaze compared to the big guy's precious little candle.

Through the lick of flames, his eyes widened. Trying to compete, he poured more intention into his talisman, and it burned brighter, but still insignificant compared to mine.

Let him try, but the more intention he used, the faster his ink would fade.

The sudden flare caught all the workers' attentions, lighting up the previously dim factory like summer fireworks. Realizing a fight was imminent, the workers ripped the needles from their arms, dropped their mixing peels, and stampeded toward the factory doors. A distant yelling could be heard from the second floor, where the foreman shook his fist through the grimy and dirty window, a laughable attempt to try and threaten his workers back to their stations.

The bodyguards also tried shouting at people to get back to work, but the shouts went ignored, and the factory emptied out as quickly as sushi on a conveyor belt. The only noise left was the hum of the machines, the growl of the oven, and the excited roar of my blade. The cantankerous noise of the factory floor had been suspended so suddenly the air held its breath in anticipation.

The second bodyguard reached for a talisman from the fanny pack worn over his armor. The kanji written on it was a blur and too far away for me to read, and I braced myself for anything.

A thin film of water cloaked his blade.

Right. Water against fire. That one was trying to be clever. Both bodyguards advanced on me at the same time.

I dunked underneath the first attack, and blocked the second, fire on fire. My opponent winced, blinded by the brightness of my katana. I shifted back my weight and pitched my opponent forward. A slash of flame severed his torso. The stench of burnt flesh singed my nostrils.

Then, I quickly turned and blocked a downward slash of water. Despite the elemental disadvantage, my ink was stronger and purer and thus far hotter. With a hiss, the water evaporated around my opponent's blade.

"I thought your clan was all gone," the last bodyguard had the gall to say. The scalding fog clouded his expression and his voice continued as a disembodied reverb, "I thought they died in defense of the capital. What did you do to survive? Abandon them? Run away like a scaredy little girl?"

My jaw tightened, my molars grinding together. The fog made my grip slippery around the hilt. For a moment, a scene of corpses flashed before my eyes—Sistahs I had trained with and whom I considered just as much family as my barely remembered parents. The stench of pine soot and sweat was swallowed by the stench of decay and bloated corpses.

Bright steel thrust through the fog.

On instinct, I twisted on the ball of my foot and countered with a rising strike. Arms went flying, and my opponent's katana clattered across the floor and slid underneath one of the large vats. The man screamed, and I quickly snapped forward and punched my hilt into his face.

He fell to the ground and the blood from his severed arms splattered the front of my kimono. I slammed my right foot onto the man's chest and stabbed my burning blade into his throat, finally silencing all of that hollerin'.

I straightened my clothes. The katana from the first bodyguard had dropped to the ground, still burning, but it sputtered out once the ink had faded.

I checked on my own weapon and couldn't see the color of the ink through the flames, but calculated there was still half an hour of ink left within the talisman. Most katanas would have melted in the face of such extreme heat, but mine was specialty made, forged with tamashii ink that made it more resilient and conductible with other elements.

A motion caught the corner of my eye where a retreating hairline dipped down from the second-floor window. My sandals chimed on the metal stairs as I climbed toward the upper level. The railing warped before the heat of my blade.

When I tried the office door, it was locked.

I dropped my weight, lunged forward, and thrust my

sword through the lock. The metal melted around the fire, and I kicked the door the rest of the way open.

Except the blasted thing slammed against the opposite wall, and rebounded back to shut closed in my face.

With a huff and roll of the eyes, I gently pushed open the door.

The office looked like an earthquake had scattered papers all throughout the room, and I shuddered at the disorganized mess. It smelled of hair gel and rank feet. A wall of grimy windows coughed poor lighting into the office, doing little to help a struggling flickering Totoro lamp atop the desk. I distinctly heard whimpering from across the room.

From underneath the desk, I dragged out the foreman by a bushel of his Jheri curls and shoved him against the window. I had to clutch him tight 'cause he slicked against those grimy windows like grease.

I threatened, "Tell your warlord that he is not welcome in this village. Also, his goons could use better manners."

"Tell him yourself, bitch," the foreman spat. Not brave enough to spit at me, but enough to aim at the ground and darken my tabis with his splatter.

I thrust back my arm, the foreman squeezed his eyes shut, and I pierced my fire-coated katana through the window. Spider-webs crawled through the glass, forming a jagged giant web that then shattered at the fault lines. Fresher air muffled some of the stank of the office. *Thank god.*

The foreman peeked both of his eyes open. Shock and surprise overcame his face to realize he was unharmed. His little mustache twitched as he opened his mouth to say something. But I didn't care.

I tossed him out the window.

A scream and splash soon followed. I watched unsympathetically as the foreman flailed and drowned in the boiling vat of ink.

Back in the day, there were many who had been jealous

of the clan and would lob the word 'bitch' at me and my Sistahs. We shut them all up real quick, but there were always those few who had to learn the hard way.

I looked over my shoulder at the huddled and quivering figure in the corner—that same punk who had been smart enough to run from the restaurant. Wouldn't want her to think I missed her. I approached the girl as she sobbed into her pink bandanna.

"Tell your warlord that this village is protected," I said a second time. I did not like repeating myself.

"Yes, ma'am," she sniveled as she bobbed her head like a lucky beckoning cat.

Finally. Someone around here had learned some manners. I just didn't understand why I had to be the one dishing out the lesson. I didn't have the time to go around educating folks. I didn't have the time to correct every ignorant word that fell from the mouths of people who didn't care to change. Nor should I always have to prove why my existence deserves their respect.

But then . . . there are those days when your patience wears thin, and the cuts are too many to ignore, when you're too tired but not tired enough, when you've had enough of the bullshit and the tomfoolery, and you've reached that magical moment when you've manifested the ability to *make time*.

Someone's got to teach these fools: Never disrespect a Black woman.

CHAPTER 6

SNATCHED

I walked a brisk pace through the streets. The sun had descended ten degrees since noon, which meant I was running behind schedule. I should have been left the village by now, but of course I couldn't leave well enough alone. I just *had* to get involved. Now look at the time. The sun was up there mocking my pace as it dipped lower in the sky.

Not only that, but the streets were annoyingly congested at this time of day. Everybody and their mommas were out doing their afternoon errands before they shut themselves in their houses for the night when the demons were stronger and more active. If the demons ever broke through the village gate, it was always better to be inside, behind the doors of your warded home, as a second line of defense. Which was why my dumb ass needed to stop playing around and get myself on home.

A guard waved at me as I approached the large wooden gate of the village. I remembered a time when the village didn't have walls, or guards, and the demon threat was a concern for someone else on the other side of the island. I recognized the guard's face as I came closer. Always annoyingly chatty, but he must be the reliable sort since he's been assigned to the gate for a few months now. I didn't really have the time to slow down and entertain his idle chit-chat. I gave him a brief acknowledging nod and continued past him through the open gates.

"Sistah Samurai!" The guard yelled.

I heard the slap of his wooden zoris running after me. I should have kept going, but the guards rarely had the courage to venture outside the gates, and the curiosity of it all had me pausing in my tracks. I glanced over my shoulder and narrowed my eyes at the interloper. He better not waste my time.

The guard nervously ran a hand over the top of his fade, with a spiral leaf symbol shaved into the sides. "One of your friends came through the gate earlier. Think she was another one of you. A Sistah Samurai."

A buzz sounded in my ear, fading in and out of volume.

"*Ex-cuse* you?" I demanded, not liking this joke at all. That was impossible. I counted all the headbands. I hunted down the clan ledger. I searched for other survivors and found none. I was the last Sistah Samurai left.

My mind raced with thoughts. Perhaps it was another samurai from a different clan? There were a few of those still running around, but more than likely, someone was masquerading as someone they shouldn't. After all, a lot of relics and personal effects had been stolen from the capital. I severed quite a few hands of those graveyard thieves myself.

In the corner of my eye, I swear something moved. I looked behind me, but my shadow was still there, and I glared at it reproachfully. *Stay.*

"I don't know for sure," the guard said, with a loud gulp. "She didn't have your signature blades, or your headband, or any of the clan seals, but there was something about her, you know? The way she carried herself that was a bit like you. She never claimed to be a samurai, but I was just making conversation and asked if she knew you, is all. She seemed to think so and said she'd be looking for you. Don't know if she found you or not, but just in case she's not a friendly . . . I thought I'd give you a heads-up."

"I appreciate the warning," I said sincerely. I would rather know what was coming than not. "No, she didn't find me. I don't have the time to worry about that right now, but if she's still in the village tomorrow, I'll check it out. Thank you for letting me know."

"No problem, Sistah—" The overwhelming sound of rapid-fire bursts disrupted his words.

The sound snapped me into motion, and I swiveled behind a tree to avoid the attack. I peeked from behind the pine trunk. The guard's body quake stiltedly, battered by projectiles from behind, while his face was stuck in a tengu mask of horror.

The village bells clanged. The guards along the walls shouted and the village gate closed. They activated the talismans, which glowed a dull gold atop the watch towers.

After what seemed an eternity, the guard crumpled forward, and his corpse landed face-first into the road dust. The ensuing silence ached. I squinted past the space the young guard had briefly occupied toward the shadowed figure crouched in the bushes on the other side of the road. That mysterious figure emerged from the dappled shade into the sunlight.

A ripped cowboy hat shaded the upper half of the demon's face. They say that demons are creatures made from the discarded parts of multiple worlds. I could almost believe it—looking at the result of someone shoving piranha teeth onto an ugly clay marionette. I've seen this particular kind before. It had a name in the bestiary: The White Demon.

The demon and I glanced at each other, and then at the fallen pockmarked corpse of the guard.

When you die, your soul is released from your mortal coil to transition to the hereafter. But it didn't do so immediately. Funerary rites were important to help speed a soul's transition, but some souls lingered or lost their way. Sometimes, they inhabited rivers and trees. Most often, a demon got there first.

The demon pounced, propelled into the air on all fours like a jumping spider. It landed atop the guard's body and a mouth of a hundred teeth yawned open. The guard's body began glowing gold, shimmering ephemeral spots in my vision, as the demon sucked out his soul.

So many of the souls that were consumed by demons would never know peace, including the souls of my Sistahs. I carried that fact on my shoulders every day, and to watch that demon straddle that corpse—I was already moving before I was aware of it.

I circled my katana overhead and brought it down with my whole body behind it. The demon pounced away; quicker than my eyes could follow. The cowboy hat, sliced in half, fluttered to the ground in seesawing arcs. It landed atop the guard's arm, still glowing gold, meaning the soul was still attached to the guard's body.

The demon landed a few paces away on its hindlegs. Without its hat, the damned thing had no eyes and no nose. Just a white face with wickedly sharp teeth. Grinning that stupid, placid smile at me. Then the demon flung its shawl aside to reveal a giant machine gun.

Shit.

I scooped the guard's body over my shoulder and raced out of the way of the bullets. They pinged and followed at my heels, creating a trench in the ground behind me. I vaulted behind a nearby boulder and pressed my back against the stone as the bullets chewed into the granite. A bullet shot through my afro poking out above the stone, and I frowned at the smell of burnt hair.

The click click click of the machine gun slowed.

I slapped a talisman to the flat of my blade. Leaving

behind the corpse, I hurdled the boulder and a rushing river sprouted from my katana. The demon was so fast, it left behind a double image for me to slash through. I whirled, WATER spouting around me like a cyclone, and the wide attack clipped the demon's shoulder.

The demon slugged that large machine gun like a massive metal club. Not much space to do anything but duck or avoid it. I backed up, and the still-hot barrel brushed across the cotton of my kimono, catching on the inside fold, and pressing hot into my shoulder. I shoulder-leaned out of the way, but the move shifted my center of gravity. I followed the momentum, changing my weight to my back foot and front-kicked the demon's face in.

The demon drifted back with a blur. Its creepy smile grew wider to split its blank face in half. Then the demon's left arm shot toward me, elastic like dough, stretching impossibly across the distance.

I dropped my leg forward and slashed, throwing all my power behind the downward stroke. Water spray hit my face and the pale rubbery limb flopped to the ground. It squeaked when I stepped atop it with satisfaction, but the demon only tilted its eerie white face and proceeded to regenerate the severed flesh into another fully tactile limb.

Before it could finish, I charged.

The demon brought up the machine gun to block my attack. I raised my katana and, with additional intention, brought the force of a hurricane down atop its head. The gun shattered. I sliced through the demon's soft flesh, cleaving it in half. The ensuing deluge of guts and water flooded the pine forest beyond.

The exhausted talisman peeled off my katana and wadded to the ground.

Both pieces of the demon's corpse began to disintegrate, and the freed souls burst forth from the demon's remains in an upward cascade of gold, fluttering through the air like a bright cloud of fireflies. All the souls that the demon had once consumed and which had kept it anchored to this world, were finally free.

I wondered if some of those souls belonged to my Sistahs. I could imagine the words they had to say to me: wondering why I hadn't been there to defend them, questioning my word and my honor, and demanding why I didn't free them sooner.

That fucking factory bodyguard was right.

I had abandoned them. And I was still abandoning them. I should be doing far more to honor their memory. I should be carving a path of vengeance through demon-kind. I should be hunting all these motherfuckers down and freeing as many souls as I could but . . . I didn't have the time.

I kicked at the smoking machine gun. A sudden gust carried the tattered half of the cowboy hat off into the sky. The demons always leave something behind, whether it be something foreign or strange, or something as familiar as grief.

I cleaned my katana of the demon's blue blood and sheathed my sword to the cheers and hollers from the guards watching atop the wall. From one of the towers, a flutter of white and gold floated down to my side of the road like some graceful crane. It was that same Brotha Monk that I met earlier today.

He raced past me to the corpse hidden behind the boulder. Without pause, he bowed to his knees and began performing the funerary rites. I stood at his back, watching the road and tree line for any more demons that might be attracted to the recently deceased soul.

I shook my head, thinking of how that young guard had been killed so abruptly and so violently. Poor boy probably didn't think today would be his last. We never do. I wished I had talked to him more. I wished I had bothered to respond after all the times he asked about my day. I wished I had inquired after his name instead of learning it for the first time now, as the Brotha Monk repeated it over and over again as part of the funerary mantra. Names have power when you acknowledge them.

I had been the one to say the names of my Sistahs over their corpses until my voice grew hoarse, even though I knew there had been no souls to appease. By the time I arrived in the capital, their souls had already been devoured, stolen away by cruel demons that now prowled the roadsides. But I said their names anyway.

I said their names before I went to bed and again when I woke up. I said their names when I ate, when I bathed, when I walked, when I marched, when I sang, and when I sat in silence. I didn't have the time to avenge them, but the least I could do was carry them.

To everyone else, they were just fallen cherry blossoms crushed underfoot.

But to me, they were my garden.

A garden now empty, and withered, and devoid of color. And no matter how much pain I tilled raw, or how much guilt I planted into the soil, or how much I watered their names again and again and again—

I feared we'd never be free.

CHAPTER 7

CRANES IN THE SKY

Wind rustled the top fros of the pine trees, raining leaves onto the neglected overgrown path. I wasn't too far out from the village gate, and yet barely anyone came this way anymore. All that remained of civilization along these roads were the wreaths of origami cranes that mourners hung from the pines after the capital fell. Thousands of them fluttered heavy overhead, swaying with unfulfilled wishes.

I wondered if that Brotha Monk was still praying over the body. The entire time he looked as if he wanted to say something, but I think I scared him off from trying. Regardless, I protected him for as long as I could, but eventually, I had to leave the Brotha Monk behind. Whatever. He'd be fine. I had someplace to be.

The other monks, his reinforcements, had arrived by then anyway. Between the lot of them, you'd think they could take care of themselves. Although, I couldn't tell you how many times I've had to save one of their asses.

They'll be fine. They'll be *fine*.

I feel you judging me.

Perhaps I should have stayed to make sure the monks made it back behind the gate. Perhaps I could have saved that kid. Perhaps. If I were younger, and faster, and my knees didn't creak so much. I should have tried harder. I should have stayed. I know that, okay? But I can't go around saving everybody. I've lived that life before. I've got to take care of me and mine. So leave me the fuck alone.

A shadow moved at the corner of my eye.

STOP FOLLOWING ME! *DO YOU HEAR ME?!*

I unsheathed my katana and swiveled to find wherever the fuck you were hiding. A glance back revealed my shadow had gone missing. I searched the blurry trees. I circled once, twice, and found you standing up ahead in the middle of the road. As if you had always been there.

Finally, you show yourself.

Leaves crunched beneath my getas as I came closer, until I could see you clearly—a figure knitted by shadows, a dark void of absence, a shadow clone that dared to mirror my image: same black hakama, same frayed haori worn down by the years, and same brilliantly gorgeous afro ruffled by every breeze of the wind. Except your hair was white compared to my grey-streaked black, and the sheaths of your blades were devoid of color. You, The Shadow Demon.

"But you're so fun to follow," you said, with an amused smirk that made me nauseous to look at. Didn't look right, for that was my smirk, my amusement, that I had lost a long time ago. Yet, here it was again, stolen by you—a demon that has accosted my shadow.

Back on that fateful day in the capital, after I had heard what happened and rushed to discover the truth with my own eyes, you bound yourself to me. In the middle of that graveyard of ravenous crows and rotting corpses, I hadn't been paying enough attention. All I knew was that I hadn't been alone since the moment I cremated my fellow Sistahs. Or maybe it was before that, during the numb work of piling corpses while their blood stained my skin like penitent tattoos. Or maybe before that, as I walked through the gates and witnessed how a tsunami of death had scattered katanas, decimated armor, and stolen lives. Somehow, someway, you slithered into my shadow and darkened my thoughts.

You have stalked my every step, nipped at my heels, and buzzed around like an annoying gnat I could not swat away. Usually, I did a good job of ignoring you, but sometimes, on some days, I couldn't scratch you out from underneath my skin.

I sheathed my katana, knowing it wouldn't do much good, and crossed my arms. I was so tired of you annoying the shit out of me all the time.

"Leave me alone," I demanded.

"But you'd be so lonely without me."

Lonely my ass. I'd rejoice the day I'm free of you. I said, mean-mugging, "If you can't leave me alone, at least get out of my way."

You tilted your head and broke my face with a bright white smile. **"Always rushing. Always got someplace to be. Aren't you tired? Aren't you tired of going to and fro? Don't you want to . . ."** In the blink of an eye, you streaked forward. I didn't flinch as you pressed into my space. **". . . Take a break? Slow down? Give up?"**

I wanted nothing more than to take a damn break. I was tired of watching young boys and girls dying. I was tired of watching poor folks taken advantage of by the cruel and greedy rich. I was tired of watching all the progress that a younger me fought for pushed back inch by inch. I was tired of leaving behind loose ends because I didn't have the time to tie them. I had shit to do, and places to be, and I've ceded that it was my lot in life to not know any rest till I was dead. Not much rest closing my eyes, either. Even in my sleep, you've turned my dreams into nightmares.

With an annoyed grumble, I marched forward and walked straight through you. I hated to do it. A freezing cold shivered through my bones every time. But you had embodied my shadow. Ultimately, you can't hurt me unless I let you. I walked out the other side of you, toward a rainbow wreath of cranes.

If I couldn't vanquish you, the least I could do was keep walking.

"You heard what that demon-snack was talking about," you said behind me. **"Someone out there is looking for you. Who do you think it is? Do you think it could be true? That one of the Sistah Samurai survived? Think she'll hate you for what you did, for not being there on the frontlines? Think she'll have any scars because of you?"**

I should have kept going, but instead I turned on my heels and snapped, "My Sistahs are dead. They are dead. I cremated the bodies. I said their names."

"You cremated the leftovers. You cremated the limbs that the demons were too messy to eat. You cremated the toes that got caught between their teeth and spat out. Did you put the pieces back together? Did you count them? Did you count all of the souls that could have been saved because of you?"

I clenched my white headband, where black letters were written in katakana and kanji: シスター侍.

That was not how I found them at all. You were fucking with me. Demons didn't eat people. They ate souls.

"I counted the headbands," I said, teeth clenched. "They are all gone. I don't know who that impostor thinks she is, but I'll take care of it tomorrow."

"Will you? Or will you keep running away? Like how you keep running away from the truth? You abandoned them. You made a mistake. You allowed them to be slaughtered. If you had been there, and honored your duty, you could have saved them. And you still call yourself a samurai? What a joke. At least a real samurai would have—"

"Shut. The. Fuck. Up," I snapped and lunged forward. I thumbed the katana loose from the hilt and slashed up out of the sheath. The shadow you stole dispersed into a cloud of brackish smoke around the blade's edge.

I knew I couldn't kill you. I've tried a thousand times before, but that didn't mean I wasn't going to try a thousand times more.

Without pause, I slapped a talisman onto the katana. I swiveled, and with a blade of FIRE, sliced through the space where you reappeared behind me. You screeched and fled more from the light than from the heat.

I stood at the ready in the middle of the road, tensed and waiting for you to reappear. I stood there until the little ink that had remained on the fire talisman faded away, and the worn paper fluttered to the ground. I glanced behind me to be sure. My shadow had returned. Maybe now you'll finally leave me alone.

Did you really think that would work?

I rolled my eyes. I've got more important things to do than to argue with you. I should have never let you mess with my head in the first place.

A ragged breath escaped my lips. Then, I glared at my shaking hands and forced them to stop. My mouth tasted both dry and salty, as if I had been sucking on sunflower seeds. The paper cranes swayed, colorful pinecones curtaining the road.

There was no time for self-pity. No time for a quick breather, or the chance to re-center myself, or to salve the wounds from your burning accusations. No time at all.

I sheathed my katana and continued down the road.

It was like my momma always used to say: keep it pushin'.

CHAPTER 8

SECRET SERVICE

You have got to be kidding me.

Dirt audibly scuffed underneath my getas as I stopped before the bridge that was supposed to get me to the other side of the river, but I wasn't getting anywhere with that big crater in the middle. I had liked this old scarlet bridge, with its red paint chipped and faded, and no longer as well cared for as it used to be. Despite being a little rough and not as magnificent as it was in its youth, it had been a sturdy and resilient landmark that had weathered seasons and endured many years, always dutifully bridging a graceful arch over the river.

And now someone had gone and destroyed it. Them fuckers.

The sabotage was obvious, looking at the destruction of the bridge. It had been completely ripped in two, an explosion of some kind blasting angry jagged teeth into the planks. Burnt wood chips littered the ground in all directions, and the air smelled distinctly of stale gunpowder.

It could have been the work of brigands attempting to ambush anyone walking down the road, but I doubted it. I took this route twice a day, and even brigands knew better than to set up an ambush on these demon-infested roads. No. This was purposeful and intentional and most likely targeting me.

Had it been arranged by the so-called samurai looking for me? Or had my actions back at the village caught the warlord's attention a little too well? Of all the days for this to happen, why today? It was as if I had started off on the wrong foot this morning, and I have been unable to get my groove back ever since. No point wasting time and complaining about it, though.

You've been complaining all day.

Shut up. If you've got a problem with it, then you can get the fuck out of my head. No one likes a backseat driver.

With an annoyed grunt, I refilled my bamboo gourd and set off at a paced run down the riverbank. There was a shallow crossing I could use to get to the other side further upriver.

It's been a while since I've had to maintain a sustained run. I felt like a kid again, sent off to run laps up and down the rice terraces. Before the demon presence worsened, this river had been a common destination of the village fishermen, but not anymore, and the trail was gradually reclaimed by mud.

If you want me gone, you know exactly how to get rid of me. All you ever had to do was take that katana and plunge it right into your—

I cursed when my foot dipped into an invisible pothole, and the mud squelched between my toes. This wasn't working. The mud was slowing me down too much, and this wasn't some weird or odd training exercise I needed to stubbornly plow through.

Instead, I veered off to follow an animal trail that wound through an ancient bamboo forest. The route was more roundabout, but hopefully, I could move through it faster.

I weaved through hardy bamboo stalks that stretched over

ten meters into the sky. Speckled sunlight filtered through the top canopy. Fallen leaves crunched beneath my getas, and deer scattered out of my way. I was way too old for all this running, really. Just as I thought the words, an annoying stitch throbbed at my side.

One day, you'll end it. One day, you'll be mine.

I could not wait to get home and get rid of you. The only time I got a break from your incessant chatter was behind the protective talismans of my house or the ones I installed in the ramen restaurant. You didn't disappear completely, but your voice dimmed, and it was easier to ignore you. You were less present, less conscious, and less aware behind those protective wards. For a scant number of hours out of the day, although unable to mute you completely, at least I had a dial that could lower the volume.

But I couldn't always rely on the talismans. I had been doing so well this morning blocking you out, until . . . the death of that guard. I guess we all have our triggers.

I focused on my breathing, air in and air out. I focused on the mechanical movement of my body, and although I often complained about how it didn't move as well as when I was younger, I had to admit it was consistently reliable. I focused on placing one foot in front of the other as the bamboo forest blurred into a scenic landscape. Eventually, the pain from the stitch faded, and the consistent pace lulled my thoughts into a calm meditative state.

I forgot how much I enjoyed this. I used to be the best runner out of all my peers, able to go far longer while my Sistahs bent over themselves, hacking out lungs. A smile tugged at my face as I remembered their expressions of disbelief as I laughed up rice terraces, jogged around mountain trails, zig-zagged the forests, and sprinted through flower fields. I used to feel like a bird. Free. When did I allow my thoughts to cage me to the ground?

Record scratch.

I slid to a stop and listened to my surroundings, searching for what didn't belong. The high rustles of chittering leaves in the wind. The domino knock of swaying bamboo. The whispers of the pulp underbrush.

Another scratch.

I turned on my heels, unsheathing and attacking with my katana in one smooth motion against the demon that launched down at me from the canopy. Startled by my counter, it kicked off my blade and bounced back to catch the bamboo with long primate arms. The demon's weight swayed the bamboo. Knock. Knock. Knock.

The demon roared.

I thrust up my arm to cover my eyes as the force of the roar scattered up leaves and forest debris. Stomping my feet to the ground, I widened my stance against the physical force. A stick scratched my cheek. Dirt splattered my hakama. Ugh. There were leaves tangled through my hair. But what was worse was the ash released by the roar that sucked out all the moisture from the air to dry out my skin and crack my lips.

The Ash Demon. I've taken out several of these types of demons in my lifetime. I didn't understand why there were so many and why they always kept coming back to harry me.

I wished I understood where they came from. The Sacred Order of Brotha Monks theorized that the demons are pulled from other worlds, embodiments of nightmares and traumas so intense they fray the line of reality and impose physical manifestations on the adjacent worlds around them. All I know is that I want all these other worlds to deal with their shit, so I don't have to.

The demon sprang off the bamboo.

Sharp metal talons scraped against my katana. It bounced back, lunged off another bamboo stalk. I blocked another slash with a bright metal chime. I moved to retrieve one of the talismans tucked away into my obi but was forced to swivel and quickly parry another attack. The demon bounced back and forth between the bamboo and my blade at a relentless pace.

Dead leaves scrunched underneath my getas as I shifted, blocked, turned, blocked, ducked underneath an outstretched talon, and parried. The metallic beat created a rhythm to our deadly dance. Timing the blow, I kicked an inside crescent straight into the demon's face and slammed the demon down to the ground with a stomp. My hips popped. Ugh. I missed that age when flexibility came easy.

I snatched the talisman from my obi and applied it to my katana just before the demon opened its mouth and roared.

The force of it sent me flying through the air.

My back slammed into the bamboo—I was going to be feeling that come morning—and I landed in a crouch, left knee jarring against the ground and dead undergrowth scratching my palm. My sunglasses had fallen beside the heel of my foot.

I forced myself to my feet and assumed a wide stance as the demon loped toward me on all fours. Leaves sprayed in a shower behind it. I stepped forward and raised my katana overhead. The demon lunged. I slashed downward and a net of black ink exploded forth to envelop the demon, caging it and stopping it in its tracks.

The demon roared, but this time, all I blissfully heard was silence.

The auditory attack rammed futilely against the tamashii ink-infused TRAP. The demon slashed against the cage, but nothing could rattle the ink-colored bars. I glanced at the talisman I had placed along the blade and found that the ink was quickly fading. The cage would disappear once the ink was all gone.

Not all demons died the same way. Some could only be killed with good steel through the head, but other required different methods of exorcism. The bestiary of The Illustrious Sistah Samurai listed all the different methods the

Sisterhood had discovered throughout the years. I had them all memorized, but even I had to admit that the Ash Demon was one of the most unique.

I opened the second inro I kept at my right hip, as the first one was primarily used to carry my calligraphy kit. The inro was attached to my obi by a wood lacquered netsuke, a toad atop a sandal, next to the netsuke of a nine-tailed fox.

I opened the inro and shuffled through the items: my afro pick, forgotten hair pins, a toothpick, a folded silk scarf . . . ah, I pulled out the small bamboo bottle of moisturizer. I popped open the cap, and it smelled pleasantly of cocoa butter and green tea.

I stepped toward the demon and reached between the bars. The enraged demon had battled against its cage but until the spell ended, nothing could get out. Fortunately, it did allow for someone on the outside to reach in.

The demon bleated at me as I rubbed the moisturizer onto its parched and cracked face. Like catnip, the demon calmed and then dispersed away in a scatter of firelights.

Then, I rubbed the moisturizer onto my face, arms, elbows, and legs. I released a pleased sigh, relieved to no longer be the demon's ashy victim. I put up the bottle, retrieved my sunglasses, and picked the leaves from my hair.

I'm still here.

Fuck you. One day, I'll figure out how to exorcise you, too. I know I failed. I know I made a mistake. I know I should have been there. I was a Captain. I should have been holding the line. The only way to cleanse that sort of shame was through hara-kiri, but I sure as fuck was not dying and giving you my soul.

Are you living just to spite me?

Hell fucking yes, I was.

Spite tasted sweet, like a ball of bubble gum. But it lost its flavor too fast, and it gave you nothing when you swallow it down. I spat the taste of you out of my mouth. Then I raced on down the trail and kept pushing on.

CHAPTER 9

LA DIASPORA

I reached the shallow river crossing. Although this was the shallowest crossing north of the bridge, I knew the river reached my waist at its deepest point. I used to not like the water.

When I was younger, my parents took me on an excursion to the beach. An unexpected wave had knocked me off my feet, and I churned and tumbled through the sea. Although I washed up a couple of heartbeats later, I never forgot the fear and helplessness I felt at being at the mercy of something I couldn't control. I conquered those fears later, with the help of my Sistahs, as I paddled while they held my hands.

It was funny the arc of a life: knowing fear as a child, to conquering them as a young adult, to going back around to fear in your older years and knowing that your initial assessment had always been right. Life was an endless churn of helplessness and fear that we had no control over. The only difference was that now, I have learned to swim my way through it.

The river was a thick pink with floating cherry blossoms.

I kicked off my getas, peeled off my white tabis, and stripped down to my underwear. I didn't have the time to dry my clothes if they got wet, nor did I want to return home in soggy pants. With my katana and wakizashi in one hand, and my clothes and belongings held atop my head with the other, I waded into the water.

The cold needled my ankles. The river was always freezing this time of year, fed by the melting snow caps atop Mt. Kuroi-san squatting in the distance. The water rose to my legs, to my thighs, and then to my waist as I reached the deepest depth. Pebbles and silt shifted under my bare feet. Gold-streaked sweetfish fled past my legs. Then something stiff wrapped around my ankle.

What the fuck?

Before I could react, I was yanked under the water.

The sun speckled the receding surface as I sank far deeper than the river should have allowed. With a clench of my teeth, I retained a grip on my weapons but released my bundled belongings. They floated up as I continued down.

I curled toward my feet, and with my free hand, yanked at whatever had caught me by the ankle. My grip slipped on something metal, like a chain. I peered below at the endless watery depths, at a large circular shadow cranking me down toward it. A demon, no doubt, pulling me toward its void.

I tugged at the chain. I kicked to loosen it and tried swimming up against the descent, but to no avail.

The River Demon grew larger and larger the closer it neared, and my lungs began to burn at the edges. It was like being snatched by the ocean all over again and I was helpless to do anything against its strength. Except this time, I wouldn't be spat back to shore. This time, it would consume me.

No. Ain't no demon 'bout to have my soul.

Except for me.

I don't have time for you right now.

I shifted Fuck-Around to my right hand, pulling it out of its sheath as I did so. I raised my arm, prepared to cut off my foot if I had to.

The water glitched, and my surroundings flashed between the bright colors of a coral reef, to an algae-green lakebed, to the dark awe of deep ocean. I've experienced this phenomenon once before. The line between realities thinned at the places where the demons appear and rip a hole through the world. Some people have gone missing wandering too close to these multiversal bubbles. Those rare few who return rave of metal birds, glass buildings, and humans with eerie pale skin.

Voices whispered in my ears, growing louder and louder as I descended. A growing choral of multitudinous tones. Some of the voices were comforting like the sweet edge of a katana, and others chiding me like a well-meaning sensei. The voices were from a thousand different multiverses—of souls who have drowned, who have sacrificed, who have fled, who have dived free—and inhabited the waters. They whirled around me with a chant that imbued my arms with strength. They gave my lungs new air. I felt buoyed by their embrace.

The chain came loose around my ankle, and I swam up towards the light.

When I broke the surface, the ground jarred beneath my feet. The river had returned to its former depth. I clawed through the water. Fallen to my knees, I clambered out of the river into the mud. Water dripped from my hair, weighing down the coils. Then I flopped onto my back, exhausted, chest heaving.

"Thank you," I whispered to the souls that had saved me.

The sun warmed the side of my face, reminding me of the time and urging me to get up and continue. One of these days, I would have to slow down and soak in all these near-death experiences and process the exhaustion that seemed to root itself deeper into my bones. But that day wasn't today.

With a groan, I pulled myself to my feet. I had to trek a

little ways downriver where my clothes and bag had collected against a fallen tree trunk half-floating in the water. I pulled my belongings from the bed of cherry blossoms that had also gathered against the trunk. They clung to my haori like tenacious leeches. I swept them away and immediately searched through the clothes, and cursed when I retrieved the soggy paper talismans folded within my obi.

Well. Those were useless now. The ink smudged, and the paper wet. If anyone used the talismans now, they most likely would not work, or, worst-case scenario, backfire disastrously. I sighed in relief to at least find that the stoppered bottle of ink had not spilled or broken and was safe, as well as the rest of my calligraphy materials still dry inside the inro. I eyed that line I had scratched into the vial back in the village. If I went below that line, I wouldn't have enough for the talismans needed to protect my house.

Was it too much to hope I wouldn't run into any more demons before I got home? What a shitty fucking day.

I wrung out my clothes as best I could, but they were still cold and damp when I put them back on. I pinned my sunglasses into the intersection of my kimono neckline. The cloth straps of my getas were squishy and wet. My hair was quickly drying at the edges, shrinking and poofing up, but still damp at the roots. I ran a tired hand down my face, then froze at the sound of rushing water behind me.

The river hadn't been moving that fast before.

I spun around as the river exploded to reveal the demon that had almost killed me. The water rained down, several drops pattering into my eyes and running down my face. I blinked the droplets out of my eyes and squinted at the demon: green skin, a tortoise shell, and hair slicked back in the hairstyle of a sumo wrestler.

Then it bent forward in the water, the top of the shell receding to reveal two giant blast cannons. I blinked. The demon was apparently some sort of . . . Blast tortoise? *Who came up with these things?!*

I leaped as the cannon blasted a hole through the forest. I rolled and scooped up a smooth rock, one ideal enough to skip across the water, and scrambled into my obi pocket, where I had left the ruined wet talismans. I grabbed the one with the kanji for LIGHTNING smeared into the creases. With a prayer, I applied the talisman to the rock. The rock wouldn't be very conductive, but, at this point, did it matter? Adrenaline beat in my ears, unsure if this gamble was going to work.

I evaded another cannon blast. Then I threw the rock toward the demon, activating the seal as it left my fingertips. The rock plonked against the tortoise shell and then dropped into the water.

Nothing happened. A dud.

Then a simultaneous flash of light and crackling explosion consumed the river. Screeching like a thousand scattering birds. I closed my eyes against the brilliant flash. When I opened them a moment later, I found the demon had fallen back, floating atop its turtle shell.

Ha! Lightning beats water every time!

For a moment, I almost felt young again, reminded of a time when adrenaline and uncertainty were constant companions. At my age, you've seen almost every demon. You know how to execute every tactic with calm efficiency. Rarely did a fight leave me trembling with adrenaline like this, as if I were surviving scrapes by the skin of my teeth with my Sistahs again. I missed them. I truly did. I remembered that dumb sense of fearlessness and feeling of invulnerability that the world couldn't cut us down. In truth, the world was a cruel, sharp scythe that I never thought could get all of us at once, but alas, the reaping came.

The firefly glow of this new demon dispersed into the air. More freed souls. Floating along the river like paper lanterns. The attack had burnt the surrounding grass and caked the mud hard. Dead fish had bubbled up to the water's surface, but the river continued to flow, and the waters soon ran pink again.

Smudged with the kanji for EARTH, I crumpled up that last wet talisman, unwilling to risk another desperate move. I tossed it into the small fire caused by one of the rocket blasts. The river explosion had quenched most of the flames, but I dutifully stamped out the rest.

I'll just have to go forward without any talismans to protect me. It wasn't the first time I had to make do with such little ink. I had Fuck-Around and Find-Out, and they were always enough.

Ride-or-fucking-die.

SISTAH SAMURAI

**WILL RETURN
AFTER A BRIEF
COMMERCIAL BREAK...**

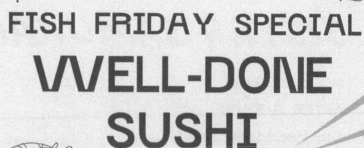

FISH FRIDAY SPECIAL
VVELL-DONE SUSHI

50% DISCOUNT

'THAT BURNT TASTE IS NOTHING BUT FLAVOR'
– LOYAL CUSTOMER

'YOU KNOW IT'S GOOD IF IT'S HARD ENOUGH TO KILLL
SOMEBODY' – LOYAL CUSTOMER

'PERFECT FOR MY I–AIN'T–EATING–NOTHING–RAW DIET'
– LOYAL CUSTOMER

EXCLUSIVE
demon drop

YOU ARE INVITED

The Sacred Order of Brotha Monks'

COMMUNITY POETRY SLAM

金曜日
20.00-22.00
BYOS
(bring your own sake)

SISTAH SAMURAI

RETURNS TO
ITS REGULARLY
SCHEDULED PROGRAM.

CHAPTER 10

NIGGAS GOT ME F'D UP

I trudged up the trail. All I had to do was crest this hill, cross the valley, climb one more hill, and then a steep mountain hike left to go.

And then, finally, I would be home.

I reached the hill's apex, stopped on that height, and scraped a resigned sigh from the depths of my soul. Of course, there would be a massive army just hanging out in the valley waiting for me. Atop the next hill I needed to hurdle, beyond a defensive line of heavily armored soldiers, stood a figure standing beneath a lone flowering cherry blossom tree. I squinted, unable to tell if the figure's blurriness was because of distance or a lack of glasses. Whatever. I've never needed glasses to behead fuckbois with a katana, nor did I need them to see that this all looked suspiciously like an ambush.

Right. The culprits who destroyed the bridge. Probably buying time to get this all set up.

Would nothing go right today? I blame myself for all of this, really. If I had just let that stupid insult slide, I never would have gotten distracted, and I never would have gotten caught up in this mess. I'd probably be home by now eating onigiri and sipping on green tea lemonade. But *nooo*. My pride had to be more important.

I scanned over the teeming throng of people, conflicted about what to do. I was low on ink and didn't dare use any more of it, but Find-Out's edge would dull before I could cut through all those bodies, and then their numbers could overwhelm me.

Did I risk dying, or did I use the last of the ink I promised myself I'd never use? In all my years, this was the first time I've confronted such a dilemma. Never before have I returned home without enough ink for the protection talismans. Without them, I'd have to stay up all night guarding the house against an endless assault of demons.

But when push comes to shove . . . You do what you gotta do.

I plopped down cross-legged atop the hill. I couldn't tell if the grass was wet or if the damp scrunch was because my pants had not yet dried from the river. The faces of the nearest bandits turned down in confusion. They probably anticipated that I would either attack or wait for them to attack me. I did have the high ground after all, but I also needed to get home before the sun set, before the night teemed with demons stronger than those I had already faced in the sun.

All those concerns and small annoyances drifted away as I folded up the sleeves of my haori and retrieved the last of the ink, my calligraphy brush, and the last stack of paper as slowly as if I were savoring the time at my favorite ramen restaurant.

I lifted the brush with the concentration of a bowman lining her sights. And then with the speed of a student taking a timed test, I wrote as many three-stroke kanji as I could. Not all had offensive properties, but I raced to write the ones that did. Each line was a confident streak of black. No wobbles or stray splatters of ink.

Once the enemy realized what I was about, that uppity warlord on the hill shouted for his army to attack. The ground trembled as the sprawling mass of bodies raced up the hill toward me, screaming and yelling with their katanas and naginatas. Still, I calmly continued my business. Nine talismans. Twenty-seven strokes. I ran out of ink and paper at the same time.

Finished, I stood and because my obi was still too damp, I tucked eight of the talismans underneath a hairband around my wrist. The ninth, I kept in my hand. I unsheathed my katana, slow and deliberate, as the waning sun glanced off the blade.

The bandits were close enough now that I could see their faces as clear as spring water.

With both hands, I raised my katana overhead and then, with all the intention I could muster, stabbed the blade into the ground. The EARTH rumbled and folded. The rupture sprinted downhill, and the ground crumbled underneath the feet of the incoming enemy. Their war cries morphed into screams as the resulting trench swallowed the front line whole.

I jumped UP and soared over their heads. The wind cut at my face, fluttered through the ends of my headband, and billowed the loose fabric of my hakama pants (hopefully drying them). It would have been nice to leap across the entire length of the valley, but the ink faded halfway there. The talisman peeled and fluttered off my blade like an origami crane.

I landed atop a soldier's face. The sound of their nose bridge crunched underneath my reinforced getas, snapping it like a pocky stick. At a shocked gasp of pain, I stomped a final time on their throat to put them out of their misery.

I turned to parry an incoming attack, and the enemy's katana shattered against my own. The tip of their blade tumbled into their comrade's chest. I continued the follow-up and beheaded my opponent in one smooth sweep. With enhanced STRENGTH, I cut through the tangle of bodies like scissors through knotted yarn. Spears splintered underneath my blows. Crushed bodies bowled over allies in their immediate vicinities. Arrows were deflected by the sheer force of my attacks.

Heat licked my left cheek. I swiveled to face the sudden jet of fire, and the flames sputtered against my summoned SHIELD. Through the hazy blaze, I spotted my attacker—a lieutenant, I guessed, judging by the fact he was better dressed than the other plebes. The helmeted opponent wore iron-plated armor compared to the rags of the rest of the army. The lieutenant's fire blasted against my summoned shield. The loser: whoever's talisman ran out of ink first.

I sure as fuck knew it wasn't going to be me.

As expected, the lieutenant's flame began to sputter. I smirked and made a mental note not to tease the inksmith too much next time. I raced forward, both hands on the hilt, katana trailing behind me. The lieutenant's eyes widened. Without stop, I rammed my still-intact shield straight into his armor. The lieutenant bounced into the air with a shout, blasting off like a rocket into the sky and disappearing with a twinkle.

The shield sputtered out, but I had conveniently positioned myself closer to the triple line of archers. Without missing a beat, I applied both hands behind the force of an upward slash. A RIVER burst forth from the blade, catching the descending miasma of arrows. One more slash and I swept all three lines of archers in a deluge that banked down the valley.

For a moment, I glanced at the warlord uphill, who was less blurry than he had been before. Protected by a thick wall of armored guards, he stood under that fully blossomed tree, shaded beneath a magnificent pink leafy afro. The elevation was higher and cooler here, and the tree hadn't yet begun to shed like the ones in the village. I squinted at a sudden glint of light around the warlord's head. What was that?

Okay. Fine. If I survived this, I promised to never leave the house without my glasses ever again.

I stepped forward, prepared to rush the warlord and end this infernal battle, but a telegraphed roar rushed me from behind. With a roll of the eyes, I turned and evaded the incoming attack with a slight lean. Another lieutenant. His blade swept past my face, close enough for me to read the kanji for 'poison' affixed to the steel. I punched a talisman into the lieutenant's face.

The surprise 'o' of his mouth was the last thing I saw before he shrunk SMALL. I squinted, biting my tongue in concentration, and slapped both hands together. Flat palm against fist holding the katana. Then, I wiped the smeared guts of the dead lieutenant on my pants as if he were nothing but an annoying mosquito.

The unit the lieutenant had been leading came at my right. I scooped up the lieutenant's poisoned katana and studied the waves on the steel. Chips decorated the edge. Poor craftsmanship and terrible neglect. I didn't dare trust this sword with my life. I tossed it over my shoulder. Instead, I searched my inro for something a lot more reliable.

The unit of spearmen thundered closer, while I picked at my hair with the afro pick. A little closer more and with the sharp accuracy of a kunai, I flicked the pick through the air.

It grew BIG, to the size of a camphor tree, and skewered the lines of soldiers on its metal teeth. The raised fist at the end landed with a deafening thud. When the pick returned to its original size, the entire unit had either been bowled over or impaled. Good thing I had extra picks at home. If I made it home.

The rest of the disparate army that I had scattered earlier regrouped for one large assault. I reached under the hairband. Two talismans left. Instead of placing a talisman directly to the blade, this time, I knelt and pressed it directly to the bloody ground.

The earth shook. A couple of enemies tripped and fell.

Then a MOUNTAIN sprouted into existence in the middle of the valley. I rose atop the summit into the air, while the bandits rolled over one another, impaled on newborn trees and fallen from craggy heights. Most died from that initial plummet.

Ends of my headband fluttering, I looked down upon that great height, as the world bowed an apology at my feet. Then I placed the last talisman atop the previous, a rare combo attack, and the recently formed mountain came crumbling DOWN.

The last bandits were entombed in rock, swallowed whole by a grave of black andesite and basalt.

The valley was finally quiet.

CHAPTER 11

BLK GIRL SOLDIER

I cleaned the blood from my blade. When I looked over at the warlord, I couldn't see his expression, but I wondered if he was pissing his pants right now. Was he beginning to regret wasting all his resources and manpower on little ol' me? Did I prove once and for all that the strength of the Sistah Samurai was as they were rumored to be and that they were not, under any circumstances, to be fucked with?

I shuffled up the hill, hand on the hilt of my katana, ready for another fight. As I neared, his armored guards prepared their stances, and the warlord's face sharpened into view. I blinked in disbelief. Wait a minute . . .

Was that a pink diamond in the man's forehead?

I had never for a minute considered that the 'Pink Diamond Warlord' would be a literal description. I shook my head. Young folks these days.

But that wasn't even the worst of it.

When Edolanta had been sacked, I hadn't arrived before the thieves and vultures picked it clean. They had stolen much of my Sistahs' personal belongings, from swords to spare change, and stripped the armor right off their corpses. I've collected what items I could find over the years. Just pieces here or there. So imagine the anger that quaked through me at the sight of this raggedy ass warlord wearing the pink sheaths of my Sistah's katana and wakizashi, an identical pair to my own—*Of, fuck no*. This triflin' bastard was intentionally twisting the legacy of The Sistah Samurai to his own selfish ends, and that was a level of disrespect I could never let slide.

I charged forward, but the damned bodyguards moved in formation to block me. Judging by how they moved, they were far better trained than the opponents I faced downhill. Each warrior had talismans ready to deploy and I had exhausted all of mine.

I gritted my teeth, knowing I was entering a losing battle. I should walk away. I needed to get home. But at the same time . . . Haven't I abandoned my Sistahs enough? I didn't have much honor left, but whatever the tattered remains of it had me rooted to the spot. I had a duty to their memory, and I've turned my back too many times.

Oh, now you want to act like a samurai? Where was this dedication when your Sistahs were being slaughtered by demons? You really want to honor them? Die like a samurai, then.

I barely evaded a streak of lightning. The electrostatic burned the insides of my nostrils. I weaved through sharp metal spikes but slipped onto my knee when the ground turned to mud. Taps of acidic rain pattered my skin. I chunked myself to the side to avoid a roaring flame and landed hard atop a sheet of ice. A metal bar rudely slammed into my pelvis. *Ugh*. I fell flat to the ground. At that moment, every bruise ached, every wound throbbed, and all my bones creaked.

"Don't kill her. Not yet." So, the warlord could speak. "I want to torture her slow. Make an example of her. Show everyone in that podunk village how dangerous it is to defy me. If I defeat a Sistah Samurai, everyone will know of me. They'll . . ." Blah, blah, blah, blah, blah. I wasn't really listening anymore.

Why keep fighting? Aren't you tired? Aren't you exhausted? Just end it. You might not have lived with honor, but the least you can do is die with it.

I squeezed my eyes shut, trying to ignore the voices assaulting me on two fronts.

How did I get here? How did I get to this moment with some fool with a pink diamond in his forehead villain monologue-ing over me? Or a demon in my head tempting me to perform hara-kiri so it could eat my soul? I should have just left things alone. I should have swallowed my pride back at that restaurant and taken my ass home. No detours, no side quests, because this was what happens when I break from routine. I make mistakes. I get sloppy. And now some bougie ass warlord might get lucky and kill me. I should have minded my own damn business.

I curled around my wakizashi. Pissed. Conflicted. Helpless. I didn't know if I wanted to live, or to die. I was so tired, and I was finding it harder and harder to think of everything I was fighting for.

Let go. Let it all go.

I had decided a long time ago, out of necessity, that the living was more important than the dead. I couldn't spend my entire life as an avenger. I couldn't spend all my time atoning for my mistakes. I couldn't fall on my sword when others were depending on me to live. *But.* I've regretted that decision my entire life. I swore oaths to fight and die a formation. I had looked my Sistahs in their eyes, held them in my arms, and promised never to abandon them.

And then, I did.

I was no samurai. I was a flaky piece of shit that should have chosen death before dishonor. The guilt ate away at me like a poison. It choked my sleep and haunted my every nightmare. A bright plastic keychain hung off the katana at the warlord's hip, and I knew the hands of the Sistah that had woven it. I saw her face clearly in my mind's eye when I cremated what was left of her.

It wasn't fair. No matter how many demons I fought or how many times I said their names, justice never came. I failed them time and time again, as I am fated to fail them now.

Was it still a formation if you're the last left standing? Did I deserve to continue life without them? Or did I deserve to fall on this sharpened sword of guilt and shame? What was honor with all my Sistahs gone?

But if I died, who would be left to carry their memory? And not just the memory of them as warriors, but also the women they were when they sheathed their swords? We used to dance like bouncing crickets around the fields. We used to laugh like fluttering butterflies in the sky. We used to roam like carefree deer, staking safe places where no one constrained our volume or tore down our joy. We made each other stronger, each Sistah another fold in the forging of our blades. Even after each of us was assigned our own daimyos to protect, nothing compared to the riotous hugs we would give one another after not seeing each other for years. Time used to feel so patient and merciful back then.

But now, who would build altars to their magnificence? Cherish their beauty? Awe at their intellect? Or should history consume us by tucking away our accomplishments and making footnotes of our lives? Should the power-hungry burn and ban our legacies? Should the warlords twist and water down our stories, and dismantle our progress one action at a time? Who was left to scream into the void and say that we were here? To declare that we were more than the soldiers the world forced us to be. We were women, and mothers, and sisters, and cousins. We were teachers, and healers, and innovators, and warriors. And we went down fighting.

The world blurred around me, and this time, it wasn't the absence of glasses. I didn't cry that day. I didn't have the time to. I had to cremate the bodies and perform the funerary rites as best I could without their souls. But the tears broke out of me now, running for their freedom. My hands shook on the hilt of my wakizashi. Would hara-kiri wipe away all my sins? Would their ghosts stop haunting me? Would you finally leave me alone?

"Bring that bitch over here."

My attention sharpened into focus.

I thought about my Sistahs—who deserved more respect, more dignity, more love, and certainly more life than the world ever gave them. I tightened my grip on my wakizashi and flipped it away from my stomach.

Fuck honor. I'll go down fighting.

My nails scraped against the ground, grinding them jagged. I trembled as I pushed myself to my elbows, and glared at the warlord through a filter of red. I had blood in my eyes that I couldn't bother to blink away. The warlord's bodyguards encroached, smug, thinking me beaten. And I was, but I think I had enough willpower to take at least one of them with me. If I could just get to my feet.

Then suddenly, a foot stepped into my field of vision: zori sandals and plum blossom nail polish. Confused, I looked up and blinked at the loose hakama pants, a haori jacket tied blithely above a bare belly, and long waist-length braids. Every time the braids swayed, hundreds of plastic beads clashed a roaring waterfall at the ends. The newcomer looked over her shoulder at me. Yellow-boned, mischievous eyes, a lip gloss-sheened smirk, and a face I thought long since dead.

"Hey, Big Sis."

CHAPTER 12

LADIES FIRST

My heart thudded hard in my chest. I stared in disbelief, terrified that this apparition was some demon who could somehow wear the faces of the dead. But most demons were obsessed with consuming souls, not winking at me. What I hoped was not the apparition of a senile mind reached down to a CD Walkman clipped to her hip, and with the pointed claw of a manicured nail, activated a kanji-packed talisman pasted across the shell.

The first beat of the song punched me in the chest. The second beat tossed me to my feet. By the third beat, I felt no more pain or aches.

This used to be *the* song, the call to arms that could rally my Sistahs no matter the location. I could feel it vibrating through my bones like magic, like a war chant, like the heavy beating of a taiko drum. A newfound energy cleansed me of my exhaustion, and I became a being of pure adrenaline, spurred on by the inexplicable power of nostalgia, a heavy bass, and a dope ass beat.

Hoop earrings swayed as Little Sistah swiveled her head. She asked, with that ever-present smirk, "We knuckin' and buckin'?"

"And ready to fight," I said without hesitation. In my mind's ear, I could hear those words echoing from a younger version of myself. With that one question, all my doubts dissolved away. She was real. Somehow, someway, she had survived the attack on the capital. The how didn't matter all that much right now, because first, we had business to take care of.

As one, we turned to the wall of guards protecting the warlord.

Little Sistah laughed. *"Is that a diamond in his fo'head?"*

"Sis, I don't know," I said, shaking my head.

"Seems kind of unnecessary if you ask me. Like, who he trying to impress? You think he cries rubies and shits out emeralds, too?" Little Sistah grinned wide, vicious, and cheeky, "Let's go find out."

Little Sistah reached into her obi and fanned out three talismans for me to take. I grabbed all three of the offered talismans. One of them had the kanji written for HEALING.

With a glance, we wordlessly communicated the plan, and oh, how I've missed that—such implicit understanding.

Little Sistah took the lead while I hung back to heal before joining the fray. I applied the healing talisman under the fold of my kimono, straight to my chest. As the ink faded, I could feel the cuts healing, the bruises dulling, and the burns diminishing. Even that incessant back pain I couldn't properly stretch out eased to a minor inconvenience.

Usually, using a talisman made from someone else's ink wouldn't be as effective as ink made from your own soul, but that was the true strength of The Sistah Samurai: the secret ritual we underwent upon commencement allowed each Sistah to use the talismans of another Sistah with the same effectiveness. Other than today, commencement had been the closest I've ever come to death, and the experience still chilled me years later. Perhaps Little Sistah and I weren't bonded by blood, but we've bled together, we've struggled together, and we've fought together. She and I shared the same soul.

Little Sistah held a small sickle in her left hand, and she spun the attached chain in her right as she walked toward the line of bodyguards with a swagger to her hips. I remembered how the village guard had noted that she didn't carry the typical blade pair, but he didn't mention the kusarigama. That was new. It seemed we had both changed over the intervening years. This twinge of worry and concern that squeezed my heart as Little Sistah walked into the fray was also new. Back in the day, I wouldn't have worried, but now I've seen the bodies of too many fallen Sistahs not to have some doubts. This damn talisman needed to hurry up and heal me faster.

The bodyguards advanced, and I wondered how much ink they had previously wasted on me. If I had to guess, a significant amount considering how hesitant and careful they were in their approach. They had certainly used more ink than they needed to, and I viciously hoped they didn't have much left.

Various magical attacks, a rainbow of different elements, were volleyed toward Little Sistah's direction. One wide sweep and the chain of her kusarigama negated them all. With impressive coordination, the bodyguards with active talismans stepped forward, while those who needed to apply new ones took a step back.

But Little Sistah was already flying over their heads.

In the air, she whipped the sickle end of her weapon through a bodyguard's neck at the back of the line. She landed and dragged the body toward her. She stomped on his shoulder, retrieved the sickle, and whirled the chained weapon toward the undefended warlord.

The bodyguards scrambled to protect him. Those who were ready to attack shuffled around the ones who weren't, messing up their perfectly coordinated lines, and all I saw were their backs. They had forgotten about little ol' me, and I smirked at their carelessness. I unsheathed my sword. The healing talisman peeled from my chest and crumbled to the ground to join the bits of frosted and burnt grass.

I read the other two talismans that Little Sistah had given me. A shield talisman and a . . . What the fuck? I shook my head with a nostalgic smile. Little Sistah had always liked to be more creative with her seals, creating whole sentences, much to our sensei's horror. It was a risky talisman, but I wouldn't have trusted it from anyone else but her.

I applied the first talisman to my blade, but didn't activate it just yet. I split an unsuspecting bodyguard's torso in half, cutting clean through bones and armor.

Warning shouts erupted around me, but not fast enough as I beheaded the next closest bodyguard. Interesting. Despite all their supply of ink and magic, they weren't nearly as skilled at close-range. Mediocre swordsmen at best. I activated the talisman and the corresponding SHIELD popped into existence, right before a burst of lightning fizzled around me.

I streaked straight through the lightning. The sparks forked and sizzled the ground. I deactivated the shield once I had the attacker in range of my katana. I feinted to the right, my opponent's guard shifted, and I slashed straight through their neck. Then I ran my katana through the stomach of the guard stupid enough to charge me from behind.

The guards quickly realized they were outmatched at close-range, as well as how dangerous and difficult it was to perform the bigger magical attacks at the risk of hitting an ally now that I was up close and personal in their faces.

They loosened their formation to create space for their attacks, but I skipped between them like a kid with too much candy and looking for more. I activated and deactivated the shield as needed to prolong its use, utilizing it just enough for me to get in range with my katana. Their spells bounced off me and Find-Out took care of the rest.

An icicle shattered into a hundred crystals before my face, and then the shield talisman fluttered from my blade, expired. A strangled cry escaped from the guard who had launched the frigid attack. A chain had wrapped around their neck. The spiked weight embedded viciously into their flesh, and then the bodyguard's body went flying, bowling into another.

Little Sistah and I had finally met in the middle.

Without hesitation, we pressed back-to-back. Our remaining enemies circled us. Little Sistah looked back at me with a smirk, and I couldn't help but smile in turn. Just like old times.

"All the ink anyone can possibly own, and they can barely hold onto their swords," I said.

"Figures." Little Sistah smacked her lips as if chewing gum, just as equally as unimpressed as I was. "I'll give you an opening."

Little Sistah's kusarigama crackled with lightning. She whipped it around, a much better weapon for long-range attacks and managing crowds. She provided the distraction for me to get close and block, parry, slash through armor and limbs.

Stop, pause, play.

CHAPTER 13

FORMATION

A new song boomed from the Walkman at Little Sistah's waist, and I found myself attacking to the beat. I added unnecessary swivels to the hips and bops of the head. A smile tugged at my lips as I danced through a confetti of blood. I think . . . I was having fun?

"Aye, Big Sis."

The kusarigama extended toward me, with a talisman affixed to the chain that tripled its length. I caught the chain above the spiked iron weight. All I had to do was glance at Little Sistah to realize what she was about. From the opposite ends, we spun the chain like a jump rope—

Teddy Bear, Teddy Bear, turn around

—and slammed it into two charging bodyguards, tripping them and flipping them onto their feet.

Teddy Bear, Teddy Bear, touch the ground

The makeshift jump rope swiveled down onto their heads, and back up, splattering brain tissue into the air.

Teddy Bear, Teddy Bear, tie your shoe

One of the guards managed to jump the chain and looked up surprised that they had survived. With extra force, the jump rope circled back around faster and harder and broke the guard's legs.

Teddy Bear, Teddy Bear, fuck you too

The weighted end whipped across helmeted faces as it retracted to its original length, bowling three over with concussions.

Little Sistah and I glanced at each other with twin grins. The remaining guards seemed to know that we were fighting circles around them, and I begrudgingly gave them credit for not turning tail and fleeing for the hills. The few that were left fought more carefully and defensively, but it mattered none as we one-two-stepped around their defenses.

Little Sistah crouched at a beat drop, evading rocks tossed over her head, and twerked through the chorus of the song. The rock thrower tried to attack her in her distraction, but Little Sistah knocked them off balance with a booty-bump and beheaded them in one smooth motion.

"Ayye," Little Sistah whooped. Then she looked at me with that smirk that knew no limits. I shook my head in turn, but her smile only widened more mischievously in answer. Then she began to sing, "Little Sally Walker walking down the street . . ."

I rolled my eyes, unwilling to entertain her mess. Haven't we had enough fun? But then again, what was I supposed to do? Dishonor the sacred tradition of the Sally Walker circle? I pulled out that last remaining talisman and applied it to my forearm. Then, I faced the last three bodyguards.

She didn't know what to do so she stopped in front of me . . .

I transformed. My skin sprouted sleek, dark fur. Claws extended from my nailbeds, and then I prowled forward with the strength and power of a PANTHER.

She said gon' girl do yo thang, do yo thang, stop.

The bodyguards stumbled back and dropped their katanas. Ah. Now they were fleeing. But I was faster. I charged on all fours, clawing up clumps of ground with the same aggressiveness and force of getting your girls through the club. I pounced on the first bodyguard, rending claws through their chestplate.

Gon' girl do ya thang—

Then I pounced to the next and ripped their larynx out with my teeth.

Do ya thang—

The third one had gained some distance. I beat the earth beneath my paws as I caught up with ease. I haven't run this fast and this free in a long time. I landed atop their back and ripped out their bloody spine.

STOP.

I transformed back. Blood decorated my face, clothes, and hair. All the bodyguards were dead, and the field was strewn with corpses. I had almost met my end and the thrill of the reversal surged through me. I'd forgotten how exhilarating, utterly stupid, and how fun living could feel coursing through your veins. With a whoop, I pumped back my arms. Muscle memory automatically took over and I danced the running man in victory.

Little Sistah rolled her eyes and smiled. "Nerd."

We looked at each other. Frizzy 'fro and half-tossed braids. Black shades and gold hoops. Ebony skin and amber. Yet soul sistahs all the same. Adrenaline whooped through my ears like a rousing encore. That was the most fun I've had in years.

We both burst out laughing, on and on and on and on.

CHAPTER 14

BREAK FOOL

"Fools!" The warlord's voice boomed from the top of the hill. He unsheathed his katana, and I admit, I figured he would have started running now that he didn't have his army or muscle backing him up.

"You think something is wrong with him?" Little Sistah asked, as confused as I was by the warlord's confidence.

"The era of the Sistah Samurai is over!" The warlord declared. "Honor and justice have no place in this world anymore. You are nothing but ghosts lingering past your time, and I will gladly be the one to exorcise you both."

Then, the warlord pulled his arms out of his kimono, allowing the sleeves to drop to his waist to reveal his bare torso. Every inch of his skin, from arms to chest was covered with tightly-packed kanji characters.

Shit.

Injecting tamashii-ink straight into the skin was a dangerous and stupid thing to do if you valued your life. For several reasons. One: The danger of your tattoo artist accidentally needling a kanji incorrectly due to any minute hand wobble could kill you. Two: The pain of renewing the tattoo every time the ink faded. Three: The need to access a large amount of (probably inferior) ink. Four: Who the fuck had the time?

Despite all those flaws, a few still risked it because the resulting magic was exponentially larger and more powerful.

Cautiously, both Little Sistah and I backed up. The warlord laughed as he watched our retreat, and then he pounded down the hill toward us, falling for the bait to draw him away from higher ground. We separated, positioning ourselves at two different angles to ensure only one of us got caught in a potential attack.

I glanced backward at the field thick with the dead. We needed to finish this quickly. Eventually, demons would get a whiff of this place and they would start swarming.

The warlord came closer. He shifted toward me, and I tensed in anticipation as he raised his sword. The kanji on his shoulder began glowing gold and then—

BOOM!

I crouched against the force of the explosion. It swamped over me with a smell of burnt human flesh and hair. The thunderous boom left a ringing in my ears, and smoke trailed from the scorched earth where the warlord once stood.

There wasn't much of anything left. Just the burnt bottom shell of his red rubber shoes and a scrap of his delicate silk kimono. The katana the warlord had stolen landed a warped piece of metal at Little Sistah's feet, of which she kicked with a sad pout.

"Idiot," I said, rolling my eyes and cleaning the blood from my katana.

Little Sistah shrugged. She said, "The tats did look cool, though."

The blast had also shaken the cherry blossom tree, jostling it from its roots and giving it a permanent lean. Burns scarred one side of the tree trunk, and all the branches were stripped naked by the sudden detonation. Pink petals rained down with fragments of diamond shimmering in the air.

Huh. What a pretty view.

CHAPTER 15

FOREVER

"Monique."

The sound of my name settled over my shoulders like a fuzzy robe. How long had it been since someone called me not by my title or familial address but by the name my parents gave me? It's been so long I almost didn't recognize it anymore. After all these years, I figured it would sound unfamiliar, but through the jazzy alto of Little Sistah's voice, it felt like home.

"Simone," I said in turn. I felt it when Little Sistah shivered with that same sense of awe. I referred to her as 'Little Sistah' because she was younger, but of course, we knew each other's names. It was required to know all the names of your Sistahs. After all, who else would say them when you die?

I didn't have much time to be foolin' around, but Little Sistah was insistent that we take a brief second to wash the tacky blood out of our hair from one of the streams that fed into the river, which murmured a gentle waterfall down smooth stones. I was having an easier time of it than she was, as most of the blood had knotted up her braids. Upside down, the weight of my hair dripped bloody water into the stream as I combed through the stubborn mats. I couldn't wait to get home, soak in hot bath water, and trash these clothes. I couldn't imagine how filthy I smelled—probably of too much sweat and death. It has been a long day.

"I could do this later," I grumbled.

"Girl, be quiet." Little Sistah playfully splashed water that failed to reach me. "You haven't changed much. Always running off somewhere. Always charging ahead. Always got to be doing something. You've got to take care of yourself sometime, and what would Sistah Sensei say?" Little Sistah modulated her voice to mimic the older no-nonsense woman. "A samurai must present themselves with dignity and honor at all times. *Now, go take a bath you dirty heathens.*"

I laughed with her at the memory. It was a marvel, really. I haven't laughed in so long and now, unused muscles around my mouth ached. Her presence had knocked over a levee inside me, and I flooded with joy.

"I guess that's as good as it's gonna to get." Little Sistah sighed as she studied her frizzy braids. They would have to be undone completely and the hair and scalp washed in order to be fully cleaned, nor did we have time for an eight-hour braiding session. Little Sistah plopped down onto a large boulder and indicated the spot between her legs. "Come on, at least we can take care of you."

"I don't have the *time*," I grumbled, even though I plodded over without much resistance. I sat between her legs with a huff.

My thoughts couldn't help but whirl over the concerns, worries, and everything else I had to do with the rest of my day. I needed to get home and renew the protective charms before sun-down, but I didn't have any more ink left, which meant I'd have to stay up all night defending my home from potential demon attacks. I felt so much joy at having my Little Sistah back, but I was also drained by the bone-deep exhaustion and the anxiety of a long night awaiting me. It probably wouldn't be tomorrow 'til I got that bath.

"Don't look at me like that. Just sit still and enjoy this, why don't you?" Little Sistah demanded.

I shifted, unable to sit still. She popped me on the shoulder with her comb, and I looked at her with mock protest. I argued, "It's almost sundown when the real nasties come out, and we are sittin' not far from a valley filled with hundreds of fresh souls. We ain't got time to waste, and I don't know about you, but I'm done with all my killing for the day."

"It's five minutes." Little Sistah rolled her eyes. "If we get jumped, you can blame it on me."

"Oh, I will," I grumbled.

I glanced at the waning sunlight. Oddly enough, carving my way through the valley had cost me less time than my usual paced stroll. What had felt like a battle stretching on forever had only lasted an hour. I was actually on time. I could make it home before dusk if I set my mind to it. It was the absence of ink that worried and pricked at my anxiousness.

And then, Little Sistah's fingers massaged my scalp, and all those worries and concerns drifted far away as I closed my eyes and enjoyed the novelty of the moment. She parted my damp hair into sections and then began braiding my hair into neat rows along my scalp. Maybe Little Sistah was right—even as a child, I was always on the go—either studying, or running, or swimming, or prowling for trouble. The only difference between then and now was that back then, I also had time for stillness. I also had time for fun.

"What are you in such a rush for anyway? Got someone back home you're protecting?" Little Sistah teased. "We're not samurai anymore. We're not at the beck and call of our daimyo anymore, but you wouldn't think any differently the way you're acting. Look at us, two rounin now."

"No," I whispered, head leaning on her knee as she

focused on the left side of my hair. "My daimyo isn't dead."

The admission brought us too close to the one topic we were both avoiding. A thick stubborn silence gritted its teeth. I wanted to cherish this reunion a little bit longer without dredging up the past and all the unpleasant memories. But we were both grown women and unused to avoiding tasks just because they were unpleasant. Little Sistah broke the impasse. She clicked her tongue and said with a level voice, with fingers never stopping their pace as she braided my hair, "Your daimyo was there with the others at Edolanta. I saw him die."

I straightened my head as Little Sistah began braiding down the center of my scalp and explained, "His son still lives."

"Ah. You're better than me, then. After . . . I was done with it all."

My hands tightened into fists. My jaw locked up on me, but I forced the words out, "I'm sorry. I'm so sorry. I should have been there. I should have—"

"No," Little Sistah said with steel in her voice. "If you had been there, you would have died like the others. I'm glad you weren't there. I had always wondered if you had survived. When that guard mentioned another Sistah Samurai back in that village . . . I had hoped it was you. I am glad to have found you again, so don't you apologize for shit." I couldn't see her, but I heard the tears vibrating her voice. "This here, it's enough."

I nodded. The feel of her fingers in my hair again. The ability to rest my cheek against her thigh. The rattle of her hair. Just to hear her voice and know that, at any moment, she could break out in song or crack a wise-ass joke.

This was more than enough.

Little Sistah finished with my hair, and we sat there, both unwilling to ruin the moment. I stretched my arms out over my knees and sighed. Then I finally asked the question. I cleared my throat first. "How? When I heard what happened, I rushed to Edolanta as fast as I could. I cremated the bodies and thought all the headbands were accounted for. I thought—I thought—"

"Mine fell off somewhere in the middle of the battle," Little Sistah whispered distantly, lower than the wind rustling through young bamboo leaves. The waterfall hummed behind us. She rubbed at her forearm, the place where she used to wear her headband like a bangle. "I got separated. Dragged off into the forest beyond the gates. I managed to escape the demon, but I was wounded and found a small burrow before I passed out." Then her voice went lower, deeper. "It didn't go down like you think it did. It was a coup by the Empress's uncle. The demons came afterward, once the dead had started piling up. But that was part of the plan too. They sabotaged the protection talismans and let the demons in to cover up the evidence. All for nothing, because that fool got himself killed along with everybody else. Now the rest of the world get to suffer the consequences of his foolishness."

"All this death because some man didn't want to give power to a woman?" I asked, almost in disbelief, but I've been living too long not to recognize the truth of it. The sad fact was that without the demons, there wouldn't be a Clan of Illustrious Sistah Samurai to begin with. Before, when samurai clans were primarily male and hereditary, they had been ill-prepared when the demons first appeared. Those old clans were decimated and there was a need for more soldiers. The Sistah Samurai began on the backs of those women who stepped up.

"Be glad you missed all that bullshit." Little Sistah shook her head. "It was a slaughter. I remember that you hadn't showed up to the gathering, and I had always hoped you were alive out there. They said you were sick."

"I was sick," I confirmed softly. I couldn't imagine what

was worse: believing you were the last one left, or knowing another Sistah was out there and unable to find her. "What did you do after?"

"My duty—or so I thought. I went south to my daimyo's estate to continue my service, but all I found was a bigger mess. The entire estate had been overrun. The family was dead. I had no master. No one to serve. I almost ended it—" she said, and I squeezed her forearm. "But my anger was stronger than my shame, and for a while, I did nothing but hunt demons in the south. Then I began doing a few jobs for the local warlords because hunting demons don't feed you."

"What about that geisha you were so fond of? Did she survive the attack?"

"No," Little Sistah whispered, strangled. "She's gone."

"I'm sorry. I know you loved her," I said.

Unlike the Brotha Monks who swore oaths of celibacy, Sistah Samurai were allowed to marry and have lovers as long as it did not distract from their duty or supersede their oaths. It was a legacy inherited from the OG Sistah Samurais who had founded the clan while holding down families.

"I'm on one of those jobs now. I've been tasked to deliver a relic to the Sacred Order of Brotha Monks. That's why I initially came to the village. I never thought I'd find someone matching your description, and after everything that happened with that demon at the gate, I knew it was you. So, I volunteered to bring the relic further to one of their temples in the mountain."

I nodded. "I know of it."

"The Brothas told me you lived around here, and I figured why not? So, I went out looking for you. It was ridiculously easy. You certainly left quite the paper trail for me to follow. Good thing, too, someone needed to save your ass."

"Excuse you?" I said. "I had it all under control."

"Of course you did." Little Sistah nodded sagely, playing

along. But I didn't have to pretend with her. I didn't always have to be strong or resilient around her. I could be honest.

"Seriously, though," I told her. "Thank you for saving me."

"Anytime. After all, who else do I have to shake my ass with?"

I burst out with laughter, overflowing with it. Joyful tears jived at the edges of my eyes. Hopefully, we'll be shaking our asses for years to come. We're alive, dammit, and we're gonna dance.

"Here, look." Little Sistah reached into her obi and revealed a faded parchment with kanji comprised of that unmistakable gloss of tamashii ink. "The Brothas have been trying to design a way to strengthen the barriers between our world and the rest. From what I understand, it hasn't been perfected. The southern order wants the northern order to see if they can figure out what is missing. I'm essentially a bonafide messenger."

It was the first time I was hearing about such a thing. Suddenly, that confusing conversation back with that Brotha Monk made a whole lotta sense. He had mistaken me for her, and if I had just slowed down and heard him out, he would have told me about Little Sistah a whole lot sooner.

I squinted at the parchment when a difference caught my eye. "Wait, is that tamashii ink? Why does it have that blue sheen?"

"It's a new type of ink. No name to it yet, and I've no idea what's in it. They refused to tell me. It can be made from love, justice, and monk farts for all I know." She shrugged.

"You think they'll ever figure it out someday? How to strengthen the barriers?"

"Men hope while women carry the world." Little Sistah scoffed, automatically. But then she took some time to think and shrugged. "The Brothas are usually nothing but pretty rhymes and hot air. When I took on this mission, at first it was just a job to me . . . But I haven't had anything to really believe in a long time, and I certainly found myself protecting this thing more than I ought to. I dunno, maybe in the end, I'll always be a samurai at heart—always needing something to protect—even if it's just a little bit of hope."

Little Sistah stood to her feet and wiped at the dirt that had printed onto her butt. With a resigned sigh, I stood up in turn. Look at me, now. The one dragging my feet.

"I know where that temple is. It's not far from here," I said. "I would take you there, I would, but I'm out of ink. I'll be up all night protecting the house."

"I received pretty good directions from the Brothas in the village. I can find it. I get it. Go. You've got a duty to attend to." She dramatically fluttered her hand as if waving me off.

"Here." I picked up a nearby stick and drew a map on the ground. "Come visit when you're finished. Maybe then we'll have time to really catch up. I might even cook you something."

"Gross. There is a reason we never let you cook."

"Hey! I could have gotten better over the years."

She squinted at me. "I doubt it. You couldn't have changed that much. Remember that time when you burnt a pot of rice? Rice! Who burns rice? *You used a rice cooker.*"

I laughed, with tears creasing my eyes as I remembered the incident.

Once she memorized the directions, I smudged the map with my foot. I didn't trust just anyone with the directions to my home. There were too many people wandering about looking to steal ink off people. "You are always welcome. Don't be a stranger."

"You're going to regret that when you can't get rid of me. I still can't believe . . . I look at you and I think this might be a trick; some demon possessing your face or something."

"I know," I whispered softly, with very much the same doubts and misgivings, but this time, this one time, I chose to believe in hope. Little Sistah grabbed the stick of her bundled belongings and swung it over her shoulder. That small action was so loud amid the murmur of waterfall and the chirp of cicada song.

"And here." Little Sistah dug into her bag. She replaced the comb and pulled out a small vial of ink.

"Is that all you have left? Oh, no. I couldn't possibly," I said, unconsciously stepping back. Little Sistah chased me a step forward and folded my fingers over the vial.

"Take it. I insist."

A knot in my throat swelled, and I felt myself choking, overwhelmed. I couldn't remember the last time someone went out of their way to perform such a significant act of kindness on my behalf. Giving up your last vile of ink could be life or death, and she was protecting something important too, with also only a little more ways to go.

"But your scroll," I told her.

"That scroll is nothing more than hopes and dreams. You have something more important to protect: *a home.*"

I almost broke into tears all over again, at how powerful that last word hit me. Some days, it was the sole reason that kept me going. It pushed my feet down the road and guided my compass. Sometimes, it was so easy to get stuck in routines, you forget why you are doing it.

"Thank you."

"We're family," Little Sistah said easily in explanation.

It made me feel ashamed. She was here for me when I couldn't do the same. "I should have been there. I know I might not have made much of a difference, but you were my sisters. My family. I should have stood with you. I should have been on the front lines with you. I should have fought with you."

Little Sistah pressed a soft hand to my cheek. Her hoop earrings gleamed in the waning sun. "I know you would have been there if you could. But you're standing with me now,

Big Sis. Nothing else matters. Let's get our shit done, and we'll meet each other home."

I nodded up. "Bet."

CHAPTER 16

BAG LADY

I finally reached the bottom of my mountain, the great Kuroi-san, that dominated the surrounding scenery. Touching the mountain's feet, all you could see were the leafy skirts of tall trees overhead. My home was located an hour up a switchback mountain path, tucked within a swaddle of hinoki cypress. I started up the sloping trail and raced the sun home. One final stretch to go.

My hip twinged as I walked up the wooden steps slotted at differing heights up the dirt slope. It was an old pathway, dotted with red torii, that led to a shrine where the villagers used to make their yearly pilgrimages. The monks came through every now and then to maintain repairs on the shrine, but the monks that lived on the mountain were recluses, and I rarely saw them along this trail. Another better-maintained trail, the one Little Sistah would have taken, looped to their side of the mountain.

Suddenly, the shadows deepened. Even with my shades on, the reds and pinks and greens exuded a peculiar contrast that made colors darker and brighter at the same time. The depths shifted and moved, until the shadows loomed larger and stretched further, grasping at my ankles, and reaching out to touch my hair.

Nope. I gritted my teeth and stubbornly plowed forward. I was almost home. I've had a long day.

Then I looked up to find you standing there three steps high, in my fucking way. You looked down on me with my own shadowed reflection, judging me, criticizing me, disparaging me with that single unimpressed stare.

"Why didn't you tell her the truth?" you asked.

I tightened my hand around my sword hilt and continued forward like a stubborn water buffalo, but you flitted beside me and followed along as if we were evening hiking buddies. Maybe if I refused to acknowledge your presence, I'd get rid of you faster. Even demons get bored eventually.

"Why didn't you tell her the truth? Were you scared she'd hate you if she knew? Would she have forgiven you if she had known the truth? You should have been there. You swore an oath. You had a duty. What sort of samurai are you?"

Each word sliced into my skin with the steel edge of a tanto, just little cuts of frustration and annoyance that battered down my patience. I tried to focus on one step at a time.

Over my shoulder, right into my ear, I heard the words, **"You failed them. You let them die. You should have been there, and no amount of apologies will ever change that. Only death could ever make amends."**

"Shut up."

"You are a terrible samurai. You are too selfish. You are too flawed. You are too imperfect. You are too scared. You are too unreliable. You are too angry. You are too snarky. You are too loud. You are too quiet. You are too distant. You are too old. You are too young. You are too fast. You are too slow. You are too impulsive. You are too emotional. You are too aggressive. You are too ghetto. You are too hood. You are too ratchet. You

are too bougie. You are too preppy. You are too urban. You are too country. You are too smart. You are too violent. You are too passive. You are too crazy. You are too clever. You are too ignorant. You are too nerdy. You are too dumb. You're too blunt. You are too poor. You are too rich. You speak too right. You speak too wrong. You laugh too much. You dance too much. You talk too much. You read too much. You run too much. You win too much. You lose too much. You complain too much. You worry too much. You eat too much. You hustle too much. You sleep too much. You struggle too much. You fight too much. You value other people's opinions too much. You hold your tongue too much. You care too much. You compromise too much. You are too rude. You are too polite. You are too fierce. You are too timid. You are too strong. You are too weak. You are too considerate. You are too careful. You are too careless. You are too confident. You are too insecure. You are too weird. You are too straight. You are too queer. You are too girly. You are too boyish. You are too pretty. You are too ugly. You are too big. You are too small. You are too ashy. You are too shiny. You are too thick. You are too fat. You are too skinny. You are too hairy. You are too sexy. You are too slutty. You are too conservative. You are too liberal. You are too religious. You are too spiritual. You are too happy. You are too sad. You are too joyful. You are too depressed. You are too magical. You are too traumatized. You are too alone. You are too friendly. You are too sick. You are too healthy. You are too arrogant. You are too ambitious. You are too lazy. You are too soft. You are too hard. You are too prideful. You are too tired. You are too whole. You are too half. You are too mixed. You are too proud. You are too black, and you are not black enough! YOU ARE TOO MUCH"

"ENOUGH!" I screamed.

The shout echoed off the trees. I spun with a downward stroke and met the edge of your dark katana with a metal cry. Our strengths matched evenly, and neither of us gave up any ground. We stepped back at the same time. We attacked at the same time. I feinted right, you feinted left. Our blades screeched in the middle.

You met me counter for counter, stealing all the years of hard work and study I dedicated to my craft. I bit my lips in frustration at this seeming fight against myself. I was one of the best samurai the Sistah Samurai have ever produced. I've led squadrons. I've organized assaults on demon clusters. I could slaughter an army in a handful of moments. And yet, in this fight, I could gain no inch.

Your strengths were my strengths. Your weaknesses were my weaknesses. I focused my attacks on the side of your bad hip, but you did the same. Our swords shrieked at each other, and the pain in that hip wailed as I blocked another blow.

Who gives a shit about you anyway? No one cares about your sob story. You are nothing. You don't matter. The world doesn't give a shit about you. They want a hero they can relate to. They want someone they can root for. They want a story they can understand—a story where they recognize all the references, all the words are translated, and every detail is catered to their ignorant, narrow gazes. No one cares about your story. No one cares about you.

Who would care about a woman just trying to get home?

I lost focus for just a moment, but it was a moment enough. I moved too slow to counter the blow I saw coming. You stabbed toward me with that dark-tainted sword, and it burst on impact against my belly, splashing my vision with darkness.

The shadows thickened into an impenetrable screen, and I could no longer see a thing. I blindly sliced at the air but found myself sawing through a sludge of miasma. The darkness suffocated and squeezed my lungs. I panicked, uncertain how to fight this unfamiliar attack. I didn't understand. How did you get so powerful, so corporal, so oppressive all of a sudden?

I squeezed my eyes shut to focus on my breathing. I had to get home. I didn't have time for this. Did you hear me? I didn't have time to fucking play with you!

It got harder to breathe. An inexplicable pressure choked my throat. In my sudden faintness, I fell to my knees. I reached into my obi automatically, and remembered I hadn't prepared any talismans with the foolish hope that I could make it home without them. Instead, I clutched the ink bottle Little Sistah had given me.

I remembered how she had given it without hesitation, and I was the one who hesitated because . . . Because . . . I still felt guilty. Because now I had no choice but to reckon with my actions and condone my mistakes.

Why didn't I tell her the truth?

"Why didn't you?"

"Because I . . . Because I didn't want her to hate me," I gasped out. The darkness tightened, folding down my shoulders, and curling my back, as if I had been stuffed inside a box compressing me smaller and smaller.

"I didn't want her to reject me," I said. "I didn't want to lose her all over again."

"What a pathetic excuse for a samurai. Only death can cleanse you now. Cut away your shame. Carve out your guilt. Bleed for your redemption. Die for your honor. And feed me your SOUL."

After a while, the only sound I could hear was my own heavy panting. I couldn't see my own hands. I was swallowed by the void. There was the pain, and the suffocation, and the migraine, but it was the weariness that pummeled me.

I was so tired.

I was so tired of fighting. I was so tired of carrying the world on my shoulders. I was so tired of pushing through, and never dealing with shit, and abandoning loose ends. I was so tired of this endless, breathless pace. I was so tired of seeking absolution for a guilt that, in the end, not even one of my Sistahs could absolve me of. If one of my own Sistahs couldn't free me, then who could?

You.

You know how to free yourself. You know how it all ends. You know that there is only freedom in death. You don't deserve peace. You don't deserve forgiveness. You don't deserve to live.

Deserve.

Deserve.

Is anyone deserving of anything? Why am I not allowed to be flawed and make mistakes? Why am I not allowed to be selfish from time to time? Why am I not allowed to enjoy my god damned ramen and come home without demons hounding my every step? Why am I not allowed to hurt or to fail? Why am I not allowed grace and mercy? Why do I always have to be strong all of the god damn time?

Because you are a samurai. Death before dishonor. That is the oath you swore.

Never abandon a Sistah. I swore that oath, too.

To keep one oath, I must deny another.

How does one determine which oath to keep? Are some stronger and more binding than others? It's a question that has haunted me ever since that fateful day. I've braided it into my hair at night before I went to sleep and combed it through my thoughts every moment I was awake. I never had an answer before, but listening to you, talking like you think you know me, made me realize something: IT WAS NONE OF YOUR DAMN BUSINESS.

You don't know where I come from. You don't know what I've been through. You've seen one moment in time, and not my growth. You've read a few chapters and think you know the end. You think I am a character in a play for your amusement. You think you know my history. You think you know my fate. You think that I am blind and that I don't see your hate. You don't know me. Nor are you entitled to.

In the end, my honor was defined by me.

And not by you.

I planted my feet on the ground. I used the hilt of my katana for leverage. The darkness growled and shoved against my shoulders. I laughed at the feeble attempts to keep me down. I threw off the weight like an old shoddy cloak. I shook off the burdens that dragged at my ankles. I stretched out the knots lodged in my back. I shed the doubts and claimed my space and lauded my own damned story.

Still. Like dust. I rise.

CHAPTER 17

FINAL FORM

The darkness fled in a sudden whoosh, and you coalesced back into the human-shaped shade that loomed before me. The sounds of the forest returned. The setting sun glimmered through the treetops. The old torii gates stood as proud and stalwart as ever, and lush cherry blossom trees lined the pathway like fierce guardians.

That's right. You have never been affected by physical attacks. You were a demon of doubt and fear, and it was about time I faced them.

"I forgive myself," I whispered. Those three soft words caused you to stagger far harder than from any blade or snarling threats. "I give myself grace. I give myself mercy. I give myself compassion. I give myself understanding. I give myself *forgiveness*."

With each word, you shrunk back, until you flung out your arms to bar me from climbing another step up the mountain.

"Stop! You betrayed your clan! They hate you for how you failed them. They hate you for how you abandoned them. They hate you because you weren't there."

"*No.* My Sistahs loved me! They loved me and I should

never have forgotten that. They are gone, but I am not alone." I unsheathed my katana and the sound crooned through the forest. "And I choose to no longer carry their deaths. Instead, I choose to carry their love."

Those cherry blossom trees along the pathway had branches that arched overhead. Across the distance, they held hands, and embraced, and hugged one another. With a gentle breeze, they danced with one another. I used to fear their weight, but the surrounding pink enveloped a shield around me.

"AREN'T YOU TIRED???" You roared, growing bigger and bigger.

The torii cracked, failing to contain your increasing berth. With a thrash, you stripped a whole portion of the forest of its leaves and blossoms. The trail bowed beneath you. You stretched and elongated and evolved into an enormous, black-scaled dragon.

Your length snaked around the mountain like a dark winding cloud. You swiveled your head in my direction, full and swollen off seven years of my doubts and insecurities. I was but a pebble to your pagoda.

"I am always god-damned tired," I snapped, unflinching. I widened my arms out in an open sword stance as if offering myself as a sacrifice. "I never have any damn time for myself. I am always rushing from one place to another. I am always fighting—either fighting for respect, fighting for more time, or fighting fools who dare to disrupt my peace. I am tired every second of the day, but I am still alive. I am still here. I am still a Sistah Samurai, so you can get the fuck out of my way. Either move or *be moved*."

I charged forward up the mountain and you, this great giant dragon, lunged to meet me. The breadth of your size swallowed the dusk and your tail curved around the moon. The wooden steps gave way to a rocky incline. I raced up and up, charging toward your descending mantled comet.

Your monstrous face rammed closer, whiskers undulating at your fierce speed, horns protruding with a metal gleam, teeth sharp with wicked blades, and eyes the color of white fire. I didn't back down. I didn't hesitate. I barged headfirst into your dark open maw.

And cut you, bitch, like paper.

Your painful screech echoed through my ears. I ripped through scales as I raced up and around the mountain. I blindly curved around the boulders and loose divots, and ducked beneath the tree limbs I knew were in my path. I had told you that I never needed no help to see the ground I've walked a thousand times before.

My katana grew heavy. My thighs burned. That hip ached. Your serpentine length seemed endless, but I refused to surrender as I carved one long continuous path before me. The darkness parted around my blade like a river of water, two winding ribbons waving in my wake. *I am too much, you say? Ha ha ha ha! I am enough. I am me.*

A burst of light flooded my vision.

And I finally cut myself free.

I slid to my knee, katana pointed forward, and panted from the exertion. The mountain air was noticeably cool on my cheeks, pasting sweat to my forehead. And yet, I felt hot all over, that type of heat after an exhausting and satisfying sparring match. My fingers had locked up around the hilt of my katana, and they cramped as I stretched and shook them out. Dusk lasted only briefly, before being swallowed by the horizon.

I rose to my feet, sheathed my katana, and looked over my shoulder.

Hundreds of gold lights wreathed the mountain. A kimono of gold silk wrapped regally around Kuroi-san. Then the souls spun and twirled, fluttering my clothes at the center of an upward spiral, churning into a whirling vortex of luminescence.

I've never seen a demon release so many souls before. How long had you been haunting this realm before we met? How many had you abused and terrorized and fed from? How many of my Sistahs had you taken from me?

The souls paraded a first line into the sky, stepping and bouncing and swing dancing with the stars. Cypress leaves and cherry blossoms swirled in their wake like second line parasols and feathered fans. The procession marched a golden arch into the heavens, and constellations glittered like diamonds and iridescent pearls at the end of their own rainbows.

I closed my eyes. And listened.

Finally.

Peace.

CHAPTER 18

FEEL THE NEED

The lights flickering between the tree trunks led me home. As I trudged closer, the light dwindled to an oil lamp glowing in the window of a stout house. A smile tugged at my lips at the sight of the rugged roof. I'd been meaning to replace the threshes but had never gotten around to it. The scent of ripe turnips and tomatoes wafted from the garden. The weathered stones that led to the doorway were as comfortable and familiar underfoot as my softest broken-in slippers.

Ah. *Home.*

The moment I broke free from the tree line, the wooden door slid open, and in anticipation, I slumped against one of the rock pillars that made up the gate. That small smile that had been tugging at my lips now stretched warmly at the sight of my husband awkwardly shuffling into his outside shoes as he ran down the front steps. The shoes flapped, and his kimono sleeves billowed as he raced toward me. He scooped me into a hug, and then finally, finally, I could breathe. He smelled of fish, pepper, and boiled vegetables, and my stomach growled at the scents of dinner clinging to his skin.

"I've returned," I said automatically.

"*Welcome home*," he said. "I was so worried. You're later than usual."

His palms caressed my face, and he studied my hair, noting it wasn't the same style that I wore when I left this morning. A handsome smile broke across his aristocratic face and his white teeth gleamed in the cloaked night. "Don't tell me you're late because of a hair appointment?"

I rolled my eyes, but despite his teasing, I swept my hands through his soft hair, caressed his brown and unblemished skin, and kissed him with all the love I contained within me. In that moment, I remembered why I made the journey back and forth to the village every day. I remembered why I faced demons every day. Sometimes it was hard, and sometimes I wanted to give in, but the fight was always worth it.

"You okay?" He asked softly.

"It's been a long day," I sighed out. I didn't think I had the energy to explain everything right now, and I was grateful when he understood that without explanation. He simply held me and allowed me a moment where I didn't have to expend any energy.

"Mommy!" Twin shouts greeted me. Two six-year-old girls sprinted out of the open door of the house, their bare feet running heedlessly through the dirt. My husband winced, no doubt thinking of the dirty footprints he would have to clean up later, but I glared at the girls for a far more important reason.

"What have I told you?" I demanded. I didn't mean to sound so harsh, but it was so easy for fear and panic to churn up into anger. The girls cringed at the tone of my voice, eyes widening and reaching for each other's hands.

"To never step outside the house at night," the oldest, by a handful of minutes, said in a chastised whisper. Her hair was done up in two afro puffs. The youngest balanced one large puff at the top of her head, tied off with a bright pink bow that pouted after a rough day.

The youngest said, scared, "You always come home before the sun sets. We thought . . . What if the demons got you?"

I sighed as I pinched the bridge of my nose and forced myself to calm down. The transition was hard sometimes—going from fighting the world and everything in it to being the mother that these girls needed. So often, when I came home, I was too tired for patience, and even when I pushed myself to make the effort, I found it difficult to convey the right words. Why was slaying demons far easier than dealing with children? The pressure of the moment jumbled everything that I wanted to say.

"Your mother is right," Hubby said, effortlessly taking over. He crouched down to the twins' level and placed a hand onto both of their cheeks. His nails were still stained by ink when he used to work in the factory to support us during the pregnancy. "You know the rules. We can't let fear keep us from being safe. I know you were scared, but next time, we will be more careful, right?"

The twins nodded.

Despite my concerns for their safety, I had to remember that this was the first time I had arrived home so late. Of course, they were worried. Of course, they were scared. And in the midst of all that, of course, they forgot the rules. Those rules would be the difference between life and death someday, but for now, mommy was home.

"Come here," I said softly and motioned them forward.

The twins and my husband all gathered in my arms, and they softened me. I wish I knew better how to comfort them. I struggled sometimes since I wasn't always here to watch them grow up. I wondered if one day they'd understand that even though I'm not always present, I wished that I could be. That I'm trying my hardest, but sometimes momma ain't perfect.

"I'll tell you a secret," I said. "I was scared, too. But no matter how scared I am, I'll always make it back home to you. I promise, on my honor."

"I know, mommy," the oldest said fiercely, after wiping their nose and sniffling on my kimono. "Because you're a samurai."

"The baddest," I confessed.

Over their heads, Hubby winked at me, and then he patted the girls on their backs. "Come on. Your momma is tired after a long day, and dinner is almost ready. Why don't you two set the table?"

"Okay!" The girls chimed and then raced through that one persistent muddy patch by the koi pond, before stampeding back into the house. I stood there for a moment, staring after them, wondering how in the world I had made something so beautiful and yet insanely chaotic and messy.

"Ready to go inside?"

"I need to renew the protection talismans," I said, knowing I couldn't truly rest until that task was done. "It can't wait any longer."

The talismans hung on the primary entrances of the property—the door of the outhouse, the front door of the house, and affixed to the fence gate. Over the years, I found that tripling the protections provided valuable fail safes if one of the talismans proved faulty.

"Alright." Hubby kissed me on the forehead. Then, he reached into his apron pocket and revealed a pair of wire-framed glasses. "And look what I found. You left them on the table this morning."

"What do I need them for? I'm home now." I plucked the glasses from his hand and dutifully tucked them into my obi. He smiled at me the entire time, finding it all very funny since he had worn glasses since he was a kid. Ha hah. There was nothing amusing about getting old. And yet, despite it all . . . Forty years was a blessing.

My husband pulled me toward him by the lapels of my haori. "How about I draw you up a steaming bath after dinner? You look like you've had a rough day."

"A massage would be nice, too."

"Anything for you, my sexy samurai," he said, and we grinned at the reference to a cherished in-joke from the beginning of our relationship. Then he kissed me again, undaunted by the dried blood or the smell of the outside clinging to my skin. I took a moment to savor the softness of his lips and the warm hearth he stoked in my chest. Every touch still felt as exciting and illicit as when we began our forbidden romance. He unabashedly cupped my backside, and I rued the demons and any other mothafuckers who dared to try and separate us.

"I love you always, my darling daimyo."

CHAPTER 19

GIRL SAMURAI LULLABY

I hadn't eaten since lunch, and that first bite of fish brought my hunger back with a vengeance. I cleaned the meat off the bones with my chopsticks and shoved the rice into my mouth. Then I scrunched my nose as I picked at the girls' favorite food, Kool-Aid-pickled radish. Hmph.

I never considered myself a fast eater, but I was always so starving when I returned home in the evenings. Hubby insisted I should start packing more snacks, but the last time he made a bento for me, I didn't have the time to eat it.

Hubby and the girls joked around as they ate at a more casual pace. Where I could, I punctuated their conversation with head nods and hmm-hm's. I was so grateful that my family respected my numb silences when I returned home in the evenings. It had taken years to get to this comfortable routine. After satiating my hunger, I sipped on a cup of green tea lemonade and closed my eyes to the steam. I listened to the pleasant chatter and soaked in the warmth that always drew me like a moth to a flame back home.

A knock came at the front door.

My family immediately quieted, unused to receiving visitors at this time of night. The youngest twin whispered,

"Do demons knock?"

I raised my hand to signal the girls to be quiet, and they dutifully zipped their lips. I unfurled my feet from underneath the low table and grabbed my katana, where it laid edge-up on the sword stand. I had a good idea of who it would be, but you never know. I unsheathed the katana as I approached the door. The outside lamp casted the silhouette of the visitor against the rice paper. Curves ranged like stylized hills and braids cascaded like black waterfalls in the inked paintings of a folding screen.

I slid the door open with a smirk. "Of course, you'd be here in time for dinner."

Little Sistah winked. "I'd never pass up the chance to enjoy a home-cooked meal."

Then, I opened the door wider, revealing my husband and children sitting at the table.

Little Sistah's eyes widened. Her gaze jumped from my husband and his impeccable sitting posture that no number of years could break down, to the twin girls who looked back at her with wide, wondrous eyes. I could see the calculations running through Little Sistah's head—their age and the timing of the years.

"Oh." Little Sistah's voice caught in her throat as understanding dawned on her. "You were sick."

"I was sick," I confirmed.

I hadn't accompanied my daimyo on that fateful day to the capital because I was too busy puking my guts out from morning sickness and horrifically discovering that I was pregnant with my daimyo's illegitimate grandchildren. It was a huge breach of duty, and I had never felt more ashamed for allowing my selfish wants to supersede my oaths. After learning what happened in the capital, I almost couldn't live with myself. There were moments when I looked at my children and felt that shame coat my skin, and I've often wondered if I was running away from it every morning that

I left the house.

But this time, when I looked at their round faces that had so much of me in them, I felt nothing but love and pride. Somehow, I've managed to build this home and create this family out of unimaginable grief and loss.

I announced proudly, "This is my family."

"Oh, Sis. They're so beautiful." Little Sistah's voice hitched, stuttering like a scratched record. She stood on the precipice, seemingly scared to cross the threshold.

I offered her a pair of slippers and encouraged her inside. "You're home."

Little Sistah burst into tears and pulled me into her arms. All the emotions hit me so hard in that moment that I experienced a momentary loss of consciousness, and then when I came back to myself, I realized I was crying right along with her in the middle of the doorway.

All my life, I've been racing against time, but for once, that damn fickle god decided to be merciful. We held each other in that doorway for an eternity, making up for all the tears and laughter that we never got to share. That hug lasted a whole lifetime.

Eventually, the tears and laughter ended, leaving behind not a raw hollowness, but an emptiness of lightness and ease. We gathered ourselves. I wiped my face and hoped I didn't alarm my family too much by crying in front of them. I turned and blinked at the sight of the twins dueling each other around the table with chopsticks. Before I could reprimand them about treating their utensils with more respect, Little Sistah grabbed a stray chopstick that had rolled to the floor and joined the battle.

"Prove your mettle, young samurai!" Little Sistah declared. She chased them, laughing and giggling around the table.

They almost ran over my husband too, but he evaded a step back as he wandered out of the adjoining room. He smiled after the kids, then looked at me and motioned toward the folded futon he carried in his arms. "I figure she's staying the night?"

I nodded in confirmation. There was no way I was letting my Sistah wander the mountain this time of night, with the darkness thick with demons. As far as I was concerned, she was stuck here, at least until sunrise.

"I also began heating the bathhouse."

"Thank you," I told him and pecked him on the lips. I turned to Little Sistah to inquire about her preferred bathing arrangements, but found her frozen, standing outside a door to one of the off-shoot rooms. Of course, the youngest would race into the room she was explicitly forbidden to enter. I'd be yelling at her if we didn't have company.

I stopped beside Little Sistah and fully slid open the screen, relieved to see that my youngest hadn't knocked anything over. I glanced at my husband, and he didn't hesitate to grab the girls by their hands and ushered them off to bed.

For a moment, we both stared into that room, toward the raised platform that held the altar I had built to honor the fallen Sistah Samurai. A full set of samurai armor, helmet and all, was displayed on the right, from disparate pieces I had collected over the years. Pink and white cloth connected the iron plates. Atop the altar sat the bestiary I had rescued from the abandoned school, which was left empty after most of the teachers had died during the coronation. The bestiary sat with other little knick-knacks that I had gathered over the years: combs with initials scratched into them, jacks and marbles, a packet of playing cards, yellowed dominoes, a worn cootie catcher, broken waist beads, a black beret, colorful hairclips and barrettes, a toothbrush of hard bristles that still smelled of hair gel, a weathered diary, and blood-splattered headbands.

I entered the room and walked to the left, where various weapons were displayed. I grabbed one of the katana and wakizashi pairs, with the same pink sheathes that were an exact copy of my own. I turned to where Little Sistah had finally stepped inside and offered her the blades. "I saw the way you looked at that destroyed katana. It seems to me you need a pair."

"I . . . " Little Sistah's shoulders hunched and refused to meet my eyes. Ashamed of something. Little Sistah was always one of those people who wore their emotions on their faces. She hesitated to accept the swords, and it suddenly felt like that moment with the ink all over again, except now our positions were reversed.

"It's alright," I told her. "It doesn't matter."

Her shoulders hunched further, and she admitted, "I needed the money and . . . I was so angry and I . . . *I sold them.*"

She pressed her hands to her eyes.

"Hey," I stepped forward. I placed a hand on her shoulder and told her seriously, "I'm certainly not perfect either. I did have an affair with my daimyo's eldest son."

Those words had the intended effect as she laughed out of her hands. I didn't consider myself a touchy person, but I think I was getting more used to it since having children and was proud of myself when I didn't hesitate to hug her. I choked when Little Sistah squeezed around my waist rather tight, and I patted at her back.

"Your Sistahs would want you to have them," I told her when she released me. Finally, she accepted the swords and clutched them to her chest as if I had just handed her a newborn baby.

Together, we turned toward the altar. Of course, we couldn't step into this room without paying our respects. I lit one of the incense sticks and we both knelt before the paraphernalia-laden altar.

"Remember that time when we took that field trip to Edolanta and we almost got left behind because you took so long eating?" Little Sistah chuckled to herself.

"Those were good times," I nodded and allowed myself to really access those memories for the first time in years. Before, when sensory stimulants triggered the memories unbidden, I would smear the ghosts away like a mistake of wasted ink. But now, I took the time to fill in the details. I meticulously sketched out the scenes. I painted color within the lines like those fancy pages in a manga. I added lighting and shading and realized that those darkened expressions of accusations weren't true at all. There had always been love around me.

"Those were good times," I said, finding a crack in my voice. The me of yesterday would have tried to avoid it, in that way young children do when concerned for their mother's backs, except I had always been selfishly scared of adding weight to my own.

I stepped on that crack fearlessly, unflinching, and did not break. I allowed my voice to rupture and shake and grieve.

"Those were *good* times," I said again, tasting salty tears trailing down my cheeks. I'd been zig-zagging through life, avoiding those cracks, for far too long. Now, I could paint a mural with those memories and smile. "I miss them. I miss that dumb magical city, too. Edolanta had the best food. Better than Kool-Aid-pickled radish or whatever the girls are eating nowadays."

"I thought they tasted pretty good." Little Sistah smirked and nudged me. "After all, the best fusions are always the unexpected."

I grumbled, unconvinced.

With a fierce glitter in her eyes, Little Sistah glanced at all of the memorabilia on the altar. I wondered if she was remembering every Sistah Samurai who held those items in their hands. "You know?" she asked. "I really hate the color pink."

I laughed at that unexpected camaraderie. "*Me too.*"

With a deep fortifying breath, together, we said the names.

We said the names of those souls who have moved on and those souls not yet freed. With every name, I saw their faces in my mind's eye. All shapes and sizes and such beautiful melanin. I saw their lives fall before me like cherry blossoms. A beautiful, painful pink. Time was cruel and it was brief. It was merciful and patient. It was fragile and easily broken. It was bright and way too fast. Cherish every god damn moment. 'Cause spring would not last.

We sat there for some time, watching the snaking smoke of the incense. It curled and thickened the air over past offerings. My knees began to ache, but I'd learned from experience that they go numb after a while. I looked at that altar, built by both love and guilt, and held my head high. I had nothing to be ashamed of.

Honor was taking care of business—whatever that business may be.

"I still can't believe it," Little Sistah said. "I never imagined you doing the mommy thing. Out of everyone, you were always the overachiever, the perfect one, the one everyone wished to be."

"Til you fall in love and get knocked up," I grumbled.

Little Sistah laughed and then said seriously, "I am happy for you. I'd give anything to have what you have. No matter what, don't let it go. Never stop fighting."

"I won't. I just . . . It's so hard sometimes. I got to fight the world and raise these girls. It's a hard thing to do both."

Little Sistah placed a hand on my knee. "Have you ever had a day off?"

I scoffed at that idea.

"I'm serious. With that scroll delivered, I don't have anything going on right now. I could get that ink for you in the morning. I remember the way. You could sleep in for once."

"I—" I couldn't even conceive of such an idea. What would I be doing if not getting up and getting to work? I automatically shook my head—even though I trusted Little Sistah, even though her ink was just as effective as mine own—it didn't seem within the realm of possibility. "No. The road isn't usually as dangerous as today, but it's still risky."

"Nonsense. Besides, there was this cute geisha in the village I was interested in talking to. I'm giving you a day off, and I will not have any arguments. I will gladly take payment in the form of your husband's cooking."

It was my turn to clutch my eyes. I sobbed, "*Thank you.*"

She wrapped her arms through mine and laid her head on my shoulder. "Thank you for bringing me home."

We sat there for just a little while longer in the presence of our Sistahs. When we left the altar room, the bathhouse was ready, where we cleaned and rinsed, before soaking in the heated waters. I didn't have much energy to stay for long. After helping unbraid Little Sistah's hair, I left to prepare for bed while she lingered to soak.

I entered the bedroom now spread out with several futons. I slipped in between my husband and my girls and kissed them on their foreheads.

I could barely comprehend the fact that I'd be able to sleep in tomorrow. I didn't remember what not being tired felt like. I pondered all of tomorrow's possibilities: maybe the family and I will visit the onsen further up the mountain, or go hiking and view the cherry blossoms before they were gone, or help with some of those household chores that have gone by the wayside, or maybe make love to my husband because it's certainly been a while, or maybe, just maybe, I'll do nothing at all.

For the first time I could remember, none of the usual nightmares plagued my sleep. No more hair-trigger sense of danger to pull me awake. No more guilt and shame to toss me from side to side. No more pushin' on. No more needing to fight anymore. I closed my eyes.

And dreamt of Blackness.

IN MEMORIAM

SAY HER NAME

Fanta Billy. Ma'Khia Bryant. Priscilla Slater. Tiffany Alexis Eubanks. Breonna Taylor. Tina Davis. Atatiana Jefferson. Layleen Polanco. Crystal Danielle Ragland. Pamela Shantay Turner. Nina Adams. Latasha Nicole Walton. Eleanor Northington. Angel Viola Decarlo. April Webster. Janice Dotson-Stephens. Tameka LaShay Simpson. Aleah Mariah Jenkins. LaJuana Phillips. Dereshia Blackwell. Cynthia Fields. LaShanda Anderson. Shukri Ali Said. DeCynthia Clements. Alkeeta Allena Walker. Crystalline Barnes. Geraldine Townsend. Cariann Hithon. Sandy Guardiola. Kiwi Herring. India N. Nelson. Charleena Lyles. Jonie Block. Robin White. Kim Doreen Chase. Alteria Woods. Elena "Ebbie" Mondragon. Morgan London Rankins. Michelle Lee Shirley. Renee Davis. Deborah Danner. Korryn Gaines. Jessica Nelson-Williams. Symone Marshall. Daresha Armstrong. Kisha Arrone. Laronda Sweatt. Wakiesha Wilson. India M. Beaty. Kisha Michael. India Cummings. Sahlah Ridgeway. Janet Wilson. Gynnya McMillen. Bettie Jones. Barbara Dawson. Marquesha McMillan. India Kager. Redel Jones. Raynette Turner. Ralkina Jones. Joyce Curnell. Kindra Chapman. Sandra Bland. Alexia Christian. Mya Hall. Monique

Jenee Deckard. Janisha Fonville. Natasha McKenna. Yuvette Henderson. Tanisha Anderson. Aura Rosser. Sheneque Proctor. Iretha Lilly. Tracy Ann Oglesby Wade. Latandra Ellington. Michelle Cusseaux. Angela Beatrice Randolph. Pearlie Golden. Nimali Henry. Yvette Smith. Ariel Levy. Sharon Rebecca McDowell. Angelique Styles. Miriam Carey. Kyam Livingston. Kourtney Hahn. Kayla Moore. Barbara Lassere. Linda Sue Davis. Yolanda Thomas. Shelly Frey. Darnesha Harris. Malissa Williams. Erica Collins. Alesia Thomas. Shantel Davis. Sharmel Edwards. Rekia Boyd. Shereese Francis. Jameela Barnette. Yvonne McNeal. Anna Brown. Denise Gay. Catawaba Howard. Talia Barnes. Armetta Foster. Brenda Williams. Derrinesha Clay. Carolyn Moran-Hernandez. Gwendolyn Killings. Ciara Lee. Letha Coretta Adams. Arika Hainesworth. Aiyana Stanley-Jones. Sukeba Jackson-Olawunmi. Ahjah Dixon. Linda Hicks. Sarah Riggins. Katherine Hysaw. Martina Brown. Amanda Anderson. Tiraneka Jenkins. Yvette Williams. Brenda Williams. Barbara Stewart. Duanna Johnson. Tameika Jordan. Lori Jean Ellis. LaToya Grier. Anita Gay. Tarika Wilson. Elaine Coleman. Reora Askew. Dorothy Williams-Johnson. Denise Nicole Glasco. Milisha Thompson. Uywanda Peterson. Linda Joyce Friday. Clara Morris. Kathryn Johnston. Rekha Kalawattie Budhai. Erika Tyrone. Shatica Fuller. Emily Marie Delafield. Mary Malone Jeffries. Mytia Groomes. Carolyn Jean Daniels. Shirley Andrews. Jameela Yasmeen Arshad. Summer Marie Lane. Annie Holiday. Desseria Whitmore. Adebusola Tairu. Tereshea Tasha Daniel. Denise Michelle Washington. Alberta Spruill. Kendra James. Charquisa Johnson. Nizah Morris. Tessa Hardeman. Martha Donald. LaVeta Jackson. Sophia King. Marcella Byrd. Andrea Nicole Reedy. Thomasina Brown. Andrena Kitt. Annette Green. Andrea Hall. LaTanya Haggerty. Margaret LaVerne Mitchell. Tyisha Miller. Cora Bell Jones. Danette Daniels. Frankie Ann Perkins. Carolyn Adams. Kim Groves. Sonji Taylor. Rebecca Garnett. Delisha

Africa. Netta Africa. Theresa Brooks Africa. Rhonda Harris Ward Africa. Eleanor Bumpurs. Alecia McCuller. Sherry Singleton. Eulia Mae Love. Denis Hawkins.

To all my Sistah Samurais

Rest in Peace

EPILOGUE

"And this is for Colored girls
who have considered suicide, but are moving
to the ends of their own rainbows."

-For Colored Girls Who Have Considered Suicide /
When the Rainbow is Enuf, Ntozake Shange, 1975

END CREDITS

MONIQUE
Mother

SIMONE
Aunt

TREAVOR
Aunt

GLORIA
Grandmother

BARBARA
Grandmother

BENNIE MAE
Great-Grandmother

MILEY
Great-Aunt

ARIANNA
Sister

ALEXANDRIA
Sister

TOKKARAH
Sister

OCTAVIA
Sister

KAPRECIA
Friend-Cousin

KAYLA
Friend

ALEGRA
Friend

MEHERET
Friend

JAZMINE
Friend

MICHA
Friend

BRIANA
Friend

Thank you for being my home.

AGATHA (AGUEDA) LOPEZ
Beta reader

ALEGRA GAINES
Beta reader

ALIYEEHAW
Beta reader

ALLMYFRIENDSAREINBOOKS
Beta reader

ASHAYE BROWN
Beta reader

BOE KELLEY
Beta reader

BRATZLIBRARY
Beta reader

BRITTANY HESTER
Beta reader

BRYANNA BOND
Beta reader

CHRISTIN JAMES
Beta reader

C.M. LOCKHART
Beta reader

DAWYONE COMBES
Beta reader

DERRIENNE REESE
Beta reader

HAERLEE_EXPERIENCE
Beta reader

JAZMINE JAMES
Beta reader

KIONI HALL
Beta reader

LAURA MONTALVO
Beta reader

MICHA HENDERSON
Beta reader

SHAD DURHAM
Beta reader

STEPHANIE SUBER
Beta reader

KYETAKU
Gamma reader

LADY AZULINA
Gamma reader

SHAE LI
Gamma reader

B² WEIRD BOOK CLUB
Community

PATSY WILLIAMS
Copyeditor

KRISTY ELAM
Proofreader

ALAYNA (_KVIIO_)
Visual Glossary Illustrator

VIRGINIA MCLAIN
Design Mentor

FÉLIX ORTIZ
Cover artist

Thank you for helping me build this roof.

Milton Keynes UK
Ingram Content Group UK Ltd.
UKHW011437031123
431729UK00004B/222

Kathrin Doeppner

Anglizismen in der deutschen Sprache